"Someone thinks I'm my twin...except... she's dead."

She handed Wyatt a battered sheet of newspaper. "I got this in the mail two years ago."

"One Dead in Hit-and-Run." The woman in the photo was a mirror of Jenna.

Why did someone think she was alive? And why did they want her dead now?

If he was in charge, he'd have already moved Jenna to a safe house and let the Feds sort it out. Instead, they expected her to meet a killer in a prearranged location.

Jenna sighed. "Yesterday I was probably the safest I've ever been. I had friends, a job I love, a place that feels like home. Now I've never been in more danger."

His phone buzzed, and he knew the time had come. "You don't have to go. Say the word and we can hide you."

"I want this finished now." Without hesitation she stepped out the door and out of his line of sight. The sound of the closing door reverberated.

Along with a gunshot.

Jodie Bailey writes novels about freedom and the heroes who fight for it. Her novel *Crossfire* won a 2015 RT Reviewers' Choice Best Book Award. She is convinced a camping trip to the beach with her family, a good cup of coffee and a great book can cure all ills. Jodie lives in North Carolina with her husband, her daughter and two dogs.

Books by Jodie Bailey

Love Inspired Suspense

Freefall
Crossfire
Smokescreen
Compromised Identity
Breach of Trust
Dead Run
Calculated Vendetta
Fatal Response
Mistaken Twin

Texas Ranger Holidays

Christmas Double Cross

Mistaken Twin

Jodie Bailey

⟨H⟩ HARLEQUIN® LOVE INSPIRED® SUSPENSE

Recycling programs
for this product may
not exist in your area.

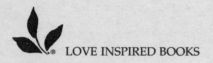

LOVE INSPIRED BOOKS

ISBN-13: 978-1-335-23186-4

Mistaken Twin

Copyright © 2018 by Jodie Bailey

All rights reserved. Except for use in any review, the reproduction
or utilization of this work in whole or in part in any form by any
electronic, mechanical or other means, now known or hereafter
invented, including xerography, photocopying and recording, or in
any information storage or retrieval system, is forbidden without
the written permission of the editorial office, Love Inspired Books,
195 Broadway, New York, NY 10007 U.S.A.

This is a work of fiction. Names, characters, places and incidents are
either the product of the author's imagination or are used fictitiously, and
any resemblance to actual persons, living or dead, business establishments,
events or locales is entirely coincidental.

This edition published by arrangement with Love Inspired Books.

® and TM are trademarks of Love Inspired Books, used under license.
Trademarks indicated with ® are registered in the United States Patent
and Trademark Office, the Canadian Intellectual Property Office and in
other countries.

www.Harlequin.com

Printed in U.S.A.

Are not two sparrows sold for a farthing? and one of them shall not fall on the ground without your Father. But the very hairs of your head are all numbered. Fear ye not therefore, ye are of more value than many sparrows.
—Matthew 10:29-31

To Christina...

More than my accountability partner,
you're my truth speaker, my encourager,
my sounding board, my shoulder...my sister.

ONE

Jenna Clark untied her bright blue paint-spattered apron, dragged it over her head and tossed it onto the heavy wood counter. The shop was finally quiet after a full day of parents and children and other would-be artists selecting their canvases and colors in order to paint their own take-home art after their visits to the tiny town of Mountain Springs.

Normally, the hustle and bustle of the day energized her, made her feel like she was infusing a love of art in her customers, but not today.

Today, she was simply worn-out, keyed up, a little bit on edge. It could be from all of the additional tourists in town for the bluegrass festival. More eyes meant the need for more vigilance. In her life, strangers truly meant danger.

"Jenna?" Liza Carpenter, the sole employee at The Color Café, leaned against a bright purple wooden chair in front of a teal blue table across the room. "I asked if you were okay. You've been spacey all day. Flu season's kicking in to high gear. You're not about to fall out on me, are you?"

"Girl, I hope not." Maybe the flu was it, though. Her brain could be wonky because she was running a fever, not because she was on high alert, praying no one from El Paso would wander into town and recognize her.

Because someone recognizing her would mean she had to turn her back on everything. Again.

She'd worked too hard to make sure being found never happened. After three years under the radar, this tiny North Carolina town was beginning to feel like home. If she had to flee Mountain Springs, it would rip her heart into pieces.

Jenna ran a hand along the polished wood bar, soaking in the peace born from a sense of belonging. When she'd moved to town, this building had been an abandoned eyesore, an old bar named Ridgerunners that had served as the local watering hole for close to a hundred years before shutting its doors nearly a decade earlier. Jenna had attacked cobwebs and cheap wood paneling with all of the fear and pain she'd brought to town with her. By the time she'd finished painting the walls with bright colors and had furnished the space with funky painted tables and chairs to express the artistic inspiration she couldn't keep from flourishing inside her, she'd come to terms with the life she'd left behind. Having a new friend tell her about Christ in the process made the remodel even more symbolic of a whole new way of living.

She hadn't been able to part with the bar, though. A live-edged slice from one of the huge oak trees that grew in the mountains above the town, it had spoken to her and drawn her in. She used it to separate the main area, where Liza helped customers paint, from the employee area, where they served coffee. The antique wood connected her to the history of the area, even if she was the newest of newcomers to the tiny little up-and-coming craft community.

"Might want to start planning." Liza shoved the chair under the table then crushed her apron into a ball and walked over to hand it across the counter to Jenna. "Even if you're not sick, one of us could fall out anytime. Wouldn't hurt to have temporary help waiting in the wings."

"True." Jenna took the apron and shoved aside her negative thoughts. Enough time had passed that surely she was safe now. "I'll call Rena and Caleb, see if they want to be on call for some possible extra hours." She aimed her index finger at Liza. "But don't you go wishing ill on us. I'd rather you didn't talk about the flu at all."

Liza saluted. "Want me to clean the bathroom?"

There wasn't much left to do. They'd straightened the shop as they went during the evening, working around the few tourists who'd come in to paint. The bluegrass festival was drawing crowds to the old courthouse, which the town had converted into the Fine Arts Center, so their typical Friday crowd had been thin. "Go ahead. I can handle it. I'm wound so tight it will do me good to get moving, get some cleaning done. Might make me tired enough to get some real sleep tonight." A full night's rest didn't happen often. Since she'd fled El Paso, sleep had been more like an estranged relative than a trusted friend. It sure didn't like to come around to visit her house.

Liza glanced at the door and eased closer to it. "If you're sure…"

Her thinly disguised eagerness dragged a much-needed laugh from Jenna. "I'm sure. Go to the concert. It doesn't start for another half an hour, and I'll guarantee Tim is staring at the door waiting for you to walk through it." Liza had been dating Tim Stewart since their senior year of high school, five years earlier. Sooner rather than later, the firefighter would ask the artist to marry him. Likely sooner.

"Don't have to tell me twice… Well, three times." Liza blushed and grabbed her thick coat off the rack by the door. "I'll see you in the morning? If the weather forecast is right and it's going to rain, we're probably going to be slammed from the minute we open."

Jenna waved her out the door, then followed to twist the dead bolt behind her. They followed the weather with the same intensity as the hikers up the slopes and the ski-resort owners farther to the west. Rain, snow and cold drove customers to them, searching for a warm place and an outlet for the creative energy they'd built visiting all of the craft stores and artisans' shops in and around town.

Mountain Springs might not have the draw of places like Asheville or Boone, but it was doing very well on its own. On the sidewalk, tourists and townsfolk alike were bundled against the cold as they hurried toward the Fine Arts Center.

A Mountain Springs Police SUV glided past. Probably Wyatt Stephens. He typically started the night shift about now.

Things outside were going on exactly as they always did. Even with the increased foot traffic, nothing looked out of place.

The best thing she could do to settle herself was to get moving, then go home to hot coffee, a warm fireplace and whatever cheesy movie looked good on Netflix.

Better yet, she could call Christa Naylor and see if the older woman would let her come up to her little mountain retreat for the rest of the evening. Christa's tiny pottery studio might be just the thing to soothe Jenna's spirit. It had worked many times before, as had some long talks over Christa's valley-famous tea.

That's exactly what she'd do as soon as she finished prepping for the next day. With the weather turning, she'd stock the paint trays and refill the bottles tonight so she wouldn't be rushed in the morning. It was likely a crowd would be waiting outside the door for her to open like the last time the rain and cold had blown in together. They'd had a rough day then. The shop had been behind from the time the door opened all the way until they locked the doors for the night. The chaos of a day of unpredictable, bad weather wasn't something she wanted to repeat.

At the counter, Jenna tugged out large paint jugs and began to refill the smaller ones they kept on display. It didn't take long for the work to chase away the creepy crawlies. There was something about the swirls of color, the order of the paints across the spectrum from dark to light in shelves along the side wall… Color filled her heart, reminding her of the rainbow God had sent to Noah.

As she reached for the next jug, her phone vibrated in her hip pocket. Erin Taylor. The closest thing she had to a best friend. Cradling the phone between her ear and shoulder, Jenna reached for a jug of blue. "Hey, girl."

"Are you coming to the concert tonight? I'm just walking in the door. It's filling up fast and I'll need to save you a seat."

Jenna unscrewed the cap on Mediterranean Seashore and grabbed a smaller bottle to refill. "Probably not. I've been off my game all afternoon, so I'm going home to get some rest."

"You are zero fun."

"Is Jason with you?" The answer was almost definitely a yes. An instructor at the army's nearby Camp McGee, Erin's fiancé was rarely far away from her side when he wasn't on duty.

"Yes."

"I'm definitely not crashing date night."

Erin's sigh was loud. "Give me a break. We'd love for you to hang out. Besides, one of the bands you said you like will be here."

"I don't know." Jenna drummed her fingers on the counter. Crowds had never been her thing, even less so since she'd fled Logan's wrath. Aside from the crowd, Erin didn't need her there. She had Jason. "The weather tonight makes it a good night to find something on—"

A creak from the back of the building made Jenna jerk her hand and slosh blue paint into a streak across the metal counter beneath the bar. She stared at the entrance to the hallway running from the customer area to the rear of the building, where her small office, a bathroom and the alley door were.

She'd locked the back door, right?

"You okay?" Erin's voice rose with concern. It had been only a few months since someone had stalked and tried to murder Erin. Her radar still pinged on high.

"I thought I heard something. Let me make sure I locked the door. It will only take me a second." Before Erin could protest, Jenna laid the phone on the counter next to the paint.

She wiped her hands on her jeans, grabbed a pair of scissors from the jar by the sink and crept toward the hall, makeshift weapon at the ready. If anyone happened to peek into the front window, they'd probably call the police…or the mental ward at the hospital.

Surely she was safe. God was watching over her. Still, His presence didn't mean she didn't have to take care of herself.

Inching into the hallway, she looked straight through to the rear of the building. The alley door appeared to be firmly shut. The monitor above the door, which connected to a camera outside, revealed no one on the back stairs.

Lowering the scissors to her side, Jenna chuckled, even though paranoia wasn't exactly funny. She glanced at the bathroom door. She'd check there, but only to prove to her brain that all was well and it could stop playing tricks on her.

The door was closed.

Her brow furrowed. Funny. She didn't remember closing it, tried to keep it open so customers would know when it was free to use. Maybe the last customer had shut it, but...

Her hand drew away from the knob.

With a crash that seemed to rock the building, the door flew open, knocking Jenna's arm away and driving her backward against the wall. The scissors flew from her hand and clattered to the floor. Air squeezed from her chest. She staggered, the world spinning, her pulse a solid, pounding thump in her ears.

A powerful arm caught her beneath the chin and dragged her upright, pinning her against the wall, her neck bent backward, pressure against her throat gagging her. Rational thought fled in the driving need for survival. Jenna struggled, twisted and scratched, to no avail.

A body, heavy and solid, leaned against hers, pinning her arms into uselessness. A mouth pressed to her ear. "Thought you could hide forever, huh?"

Jenna whimpered, pain and fear flashing hot and melting her joints. Tears stung her eyes. This was not Logan, but he'd found her. Somehow, he'd found her.

The man jerked her chin higher with his forearm. Something solid and horrifyingly familiar gouged into her ribs.

The barrel of a pistol.

His voice hissed hot against her ear. "I know someone who's going to be very, very happy to see you, Ms. Brady."

Her real name. Jenna's eyes drifted shut, and she whimpered despite the forearm crushing her throat. There was no doubt he knew who she was, and no doubt Logan had put a price on her head for leaving him.

* * *

Officer Wyatt Stephens turned onto Valley Street and cranked the heat. The air in his patrol SUV was taking forever to warm, the damp chill of a January evening proving to be one of the toughest enemies in Mountain Springs.

His gut sank. Not as tough as the real enemy seeking to encroach on the town he'd grown up in and loved. The box truck they'd located on the old Gaskins property on Overton Road a few months earlier had reeked of body odor and long-term living. It was clear several people had been forced to call the cramped space home for quite a while, but the truck had been empty by the time a couple of deer hunters had stumbled upon it.

Someone had tried to move people through town like cargo.

The FBI and the Department of Homeland Security had completed their investigation last month, concluding the traffickers had broken down while passing through, but Wyatt wasn't so certain. *Lord, please don't let them be looking to use Mountain Springs as a depot.*

It was his biggest fear. He would lie awake at night considering the horrors of someone using the tiny town as a stop on the trafficking pipeline that ran from the country's northern border to its southern border. For months, he'd eyed every stranger in town with suspicion. He had even taken a closer look at some of the families of the old-timers who'd once run moonshine along these ridges. The very idea someone would treat a human being like a commodity made him nauseous.

The idea someone so vile and heartless might be a person he actually knew—

The ringing of his cell phone jerked him out of a dark reverie. Erin. His cousin was always good for a smile.

She'd been living at his house since she'd left her father's house in the fall, and was preparing to marry her fiancé, who also happened to be his closest friend.

She probably had another wedding assignment for him. As the best man, his to-do list grew every day. He punched the answer button on his Bluetooth. "I'm on duty, E. I can't be running your wedding errands right now."

"Where are you?"

The frantic tone of her voice had his foot easing to the brake pedal, and he cast his eyes to the rearview to see how quickly he could make a U-turn and get to the house. No, to downtown. She was supposed to be at the Fine Arts Center with Jason. "What's going on? Are you okay?"

"It's Jenna."

Wyatt's mouth tightened into a grim line and he hung the U-turn, headed toward downtown and the strip of historic buildings along the main street. Jenna Clark wasn't high on his list of likable personalities, but she was Erin's best friend. "Talk to me."

"I think someone's broken in to the store and she's there. She set the phone on the counter to walk to the back and check on a noise, then I heard a crash, her scream and a man's voice. I—I can't tell what they're saying."

"Stay away from the store. Tell Jason not to go in, either. I mean it. I know him. He'll try." Wyatt's foot dug into the accelerator, and the engine roared as it tackled the hill toward downtown. He might not trust Jenna Clark, but if she was in danger… "Hang up the phone. Call 911 and get them rolling. I'll radio in from my end." He killed the call and took a right onto Barnett Street, reaching for his radio. One other officer was on duty in town for the night, but their calls would bring in the county as backup.

His headlights swept across the alley as he turned in. Jenna's small crossover sat close to the back door, but a dark late-model sports car with Texas plates was parked slightly behind hers at an angle calculated to prevent her from backing out.

Adrenaline crashed into his system, thrumming through his veins. This was no break-in. Blocking her vehicle was targeted. And those Texas plates? The same state as the box truck on Overton Road. The odds the two were connected were slim, but if traffickers were in the area and one had stumbled upon Jenna or Liza alone at the shop in the dark of the evening…

His throat tightened and he rolled in behind the unfamiliar vehicle, cutting off its escape route. After notifying Dispatch, Wyatt eased out of his SUV, eyes on the door of the shop, hand resting on the pistol at his side. An attacker would never try to take Jenna or Liza out the front door, not with so many people flowing past on their way to tonight's concert. They'd head straight out the back, directly toward him.

He inhaled deeply, steadying his nerves. He'd hated approaching situations with no intel ever since his very first domestic call when he was a rookie cop. There'd been five first responders in the small yard, a mix of town and county officers, pinned down by shotgun blasts. While he'd been in numerous firefights during his enlistment in the army, being an untested cop taking fire on home soil had sent him into a tailspin that still echoed in his emotions.

But they couldn't today. Not if he was going to deal successfully with whatever was behind Jenna's door. *You're in control, Stephens. You know he's here. He has no idea you're waiting. You have the upper hand.*

Maybe Jenna had a friend visiting, someone who'd surprised her. Though she'd never mentioned exactly where she'd lived before moving to Mountain Springs, her drawl tilted toward the Deep South.

Maybe to Texas.

Even with the vague hope this was all a misunderstanding, he couldn't let down his guard. Assumptions could get a man—or a woman—killed.

So could acting too quickly. As much as he wanted to bust in alone to make certain Jenna was safe, smart training told him to wait for backup. He approached the door from the left, where it would open out should anyone leave.

A crash echoed through the alley as the door burst open and a man shoved through a couple of feet from Wyatt's position.

Wyatt jumped back and took aim but the man was dragging Jenna by the throat and blocked any chance at a clean shot.

Kicking and fighting, Jenna clawed at her assailant's thick muscled arm. Her wide-eyed gaze scanned the alley before she spotted Wyatt, froze, then renewed her struggle.

The fear in her eyes ripped through him. He had to rescue her.

Busy with Jenna, the other man hadn't seen Wyatt or his patrol vehicle. Thankfully, the man also didn't appear to have a weapon out, though one peeked from beneath his jacket at his hip.

Surprise would be the best offense and would keep him from drawing his weapon. As Wyatt prepared to make his presence known, he nodded once at Jenna then holstered his pistol. It was a risky move, but he had a better shot of keeping Jenna safe if he could wrestle the stranger to the ground than if he drew a weapon and instigated a shoot-out with her in the middle.

Sirens sounded in the distance, from the direction of the police station.

The man hesitated and was still facing away from Wyatt. His hold on Jenna relaxed.

Now.

Wyatt dove from his position, crashing into the assailant's lower back and driving both him and Jenna into the side of the car.

Her cry of pain mingled with a deeper angry curse. The stranger's grip on Jenna loosened as he whirled toward Wyatt, fists in front of him, prepared to fight.

Wyatt was more than ready. He swung an uppercut to the man's thick jaw, staggering him backward. "Jenna! Get inside and lock the door!" If she was still within reach, her attacker likely wouldn't think twice about lunging for her, either for leverage against Wyatt or to attempt an escape.

She didn't hesitate, disappearing behind Wyatt as he kept a wary eye on his opponent.

With Jenna out of the way, Wyatt reached for his pistol, but the man turned and ran for the entrance to the alley, ducking around the corner as Wyatt took off in pursuit.

The suspect hit the main street before Wyatt and blended into the crowd flowing toward the Fine Arts Center. In the shadowy light from the ancient streetlights, he melted into the small sea of humanity.

Wyatt skidded to a halt. He could give chase, but doing so would risk a shoot-out on a busy street and would leave Jenna unprotected. She had to be priority number one.

Releasing his grip on the pistol in his holster, Wyatt turned and jogged to the alley, speaking into his shoulder radio as he headed to the shop to check on Jenna. "Suspect on foot, headed west on Main Street." He ran through a quick description of the man, which ended as he reached the heavy metal back door of Jenna's shop.

He pounded on the door. "Jenna! It's Wyatt!" A soft shuffling came from inside, and he stepped away so she could better see him through the camera situated above the door.

After a moment, the door swung outward, and Jenna stood silhouetted in the light from the front of the store before she slowly sank to the floor.

TWO

Headlights swept through the windshield of Wyatt's police SUV as a car turned onto Barnett Street and cruised past the light where Jenna and Wyatt were stopped.

She turned her head away from the light, toward Wyatt, away from whoever was driving the car. She'd been spotted tonight. Recognized. If the intruder in her shop had called in reinforcements, it was only a matter of time before she was surrounded and dragged to El Paso and the man she feared, the life she despised.

Logan Cutter had appeared to be everything a girl like Jenna could want. Well, everything a girl like Genevieve Brady—her birth name—could want. After never knowing who her father was and growing up with a mother who tried to live a fantasy before she eventually committed suicide, there had never been a father figure, other than one man, Anthony Reynolds, her mother's boyfriend when Jenna was seven. He'd treated Jenna and her twin sister, Amy, as his own... until her mother had abruptly booted him from their lives in less than a year.

Desperate to be loved, she'd given Logan everything she had and had accepted his jealousy and anger as the price of being with him. Then she'd discovered evidence of his unfaithfulness, of the levels of his depravity…

One night, in confusion and grief, she had packed a bag and fled. He found her before daybreak. Beat her. Apologized. Held her as she cried.

She stayed.

The second time was worse.

And the third… Jenna glanced at Wyatt and squeezed herself tighter against the seat. She'd nearly died after the third time and still bore scars that sometimes ached in the cold.

That night, Genevieve Brady had disappeared from Del Sol Medical Center with Anthony's help. Three days later, Jenna Clark became the newest resident of Mountain Springs, North Carolina. Thanks to her mother's ex—who had built an underground business out of making both the innocent and the guilty disappear—every link to her past was severed and she had the paperwork to lend credence to her new identity. All she had left of her old self was her love of art and a "go bag" hidden in the attic crawlspace at her apartment, insurance in case Jenna Clark ever needed to disappear as well.

The scars on her back ached at the memory, and Jenna clamped her teeth on a whimper she would never let Wyatt Stephens hear. It was bad enough he'd already seen her at her weakest. Her cheeks were still hot with embarrassment in the midst of her fear. He'd likely saved her life tonight, and the minute he'd returned for her, she'd collapsed in a heap like some weak woman in a 1940s melodrama. She was stronger than a fainting starlet.

For the moment, though, embarrassment was probably a whole lot less detrimental to her mental health than fear would be. Thinking about Wyatt having to haul her into his arms and carry her into her office was easier than coming to grips with the truth. Her logical next move was to be gone by sunrise.

The best thing to do was to keep her focus on the man beside her, not on the one who hounded her nightmares.

"You didn't have to drive me home." His presence made escape harder. Her apartment was across the street and two blocks away from the shop, above Higher Grounds Coffee Bar, another former town watering hole.

The light turned green, highlighting his face with shadows that deepened the blue of Wyatt's eyes and sharpened the cut of his jawline. His dark brown hair was tousled from his earlier scuffle. For the briefest of moments, he looked at her almost as though he might feel a bit of compassion, but then he turned away and made the left onto Main Street. "First of all, after what happened tonight, nobody's letting you walk home by yourself, especially not in the dark." He jerked his thumb over his shoulder, where Erin and her fiancé, Jason Barnes, followed in Jason's pickup. "Second, I'm not interested in the lecture I'd get from Erin if I even dared to suggest you walk home unescorted." He held up three fingers before resting his hand on the steering wheel. "Third, I have to ask some questions in order to do paperwork. And a bonus fourth thing, you promised me coffee. I don't turn my back on free coffee. Ever."

"Not even from me?" The man had never liked her. While Erin was her closest friend, and also happened to be Wyatt's cousin, Wyatt had always kept Jenna at a distance, eyeing her with the kind of suspicion that made her feel like he could read all of her darkest secrets... and there were definitely plenty of those. Jenna avoided him, didn't talk to him if she could help it. Something inside her rankled at the sight of him.

When she was forced to speak to him, her words always came out antagonistic, even when she tried to be nice. Even the shortest conversation with the town's most popular police officer made everything worse. Wyatt Stephens unsettled her insides. There was no other way to say it.

His grip on the steering wheel tightened, and his jaw quirked to the side as though he'd tensed it until it ached. Finally, he relaxed and his Adam's apple bobbed as he swallowed. "You've been through the wringer tonight, okay? We've got every available officer out looking, even the ones off duty. You have a lot of friends in Mountain Springs who want to see this guy caught. Until then, let's concentrate on getting you home, where it's safe."

Safe. The word no longer had meaning. Jenna sighed and stared out the window into the side mirror at Jason's headlights behind them as Wyatt cruised slowly along the street. He had no idea what he was talking about. Nowhere in town was safe. She hadn't flown far enough from Texas. Somehow, after three years, Logan's men had found her in the town she now called home.

She'd grown to love this place in a way she'd never

imagined possible. The local bookstore, staffed by volunteers from the library, glided past. The co-op where local artists consigned their paintings, pottery and other art. Higher Grounds Coffee Bar…

She leaned closer to the window so she could see the second story of the building. Her apartment. The place where she'd once felt safe. She'd been taught to defend herself after all…and she'd failed. "I should have been able to handle the guy tonight."

"What?"

This was what bothered her, the slight shame that had dogged her for the past hour. "My mom had a boyfriend, Anthony. He—he took care of me and my sister, taught us how to take care of ourselves." She smiled slightly at the memory. "Taught us how to break away if a guy ever tried to grab us. Said the worst thing we could do was kick or knee, because it would throw us off balance. 'Poke him in the eye,' he said. 'Fight like a girl.' He said girls are tougher than most guys think they are, so fighting like a girl was a good thing." Jenna sniffed, Anthony's voice clear in her head, even though everything he'd taught her had flown right out of her head in the panic of reality.

"'Fight like a girl,'" Wyatt murmured, making the turn into the alley by her apartment. "I'll have to remember your story, maybe teach it to Erin."

"I'm sure Erin can take care of herself." The way Jenna was going to have to as soon as she could flee.

When the SUV came to a stop, Jenna shoved out the door, keys in hand, mind focused on getting away from her protectors and into the attic so she could grab her packed bag and get out of town. Her heart pounded, her feet desperate to carry her up the metal stairs on the outside of the building. First, she'd make her entourage leave, then she would barricade herself in and find the gun she'd shoved into the darkest, farthest corner of her closet shelf…

The stairs vibrated as Wyatt pounded up with Erin and Jason close behind. He extracted the keys from Jenna's hand as she aimed for the door, gently slipping between her and the entry. "I'm going in first."

Jenna wanted to argue, but her throat closed as Wyatt turned the key in the lock and pushed open the door, drawing his pistol as he pocketed her keys.

Someone could be in her home, waiting for her. It wasn't a foreign idea, but watching Wyatt slip into her front door armed…

Jason edged in front of Jenna and stood inside the doorway as Erin's arm slipped around her waist and guided her toward the threshold. "Come on. Let's stand inside."

Inside. So no one on the outside would see her.

Tremors shook Jenna by the time Wyatt walked along the short hallway leading to her bedroom. He holstered his pistol, his broad shoulders seeming to dwarf the space. He'd never been in her apartment before, and his presence served to make an already surreal night even more bizarre. "All clear."

Three sets of eyes turned to Jenna, who stood between her living room and the bar that separated the area from the kitchen, her feet rooted to the polished hardwood. This must be what zoo animals felt like. On display. Exposed. Vulnerable.

Those were feelings she'd vowed never to succumb to again. Lifting her chin, she turned her focus to Jason and Erin and slipped behind the mask she'd worn for years. They'd be the easiest ones to convince. "You guys didn't have to follow me home. I know you were looking forward to the concerts tonight. Go. I'm fine. Really. Plus, I'll be a whole lot better if I don't have an audience staring at me while I put together the pieces of somebody breaking in to my shop."

"Not just breaking in to your shop. He—" Erin stopped abruptly as Jason laid a hand on her back, his fingers grazing her shoulder-length brown hair. She clamped her mouth shut, opened it again, then leaned against Jason's chest and let him slide his arm around her waist. "I'm sorry. It's just, after what happened to us…" She sighed. "I'm sure tonight terrified you, but I'm also sure nobody's stalking you like they were me. I shouldn't have hinted at such a thing."

Good. Let them all think the attack was a one-off and she was merely in the wrong place at the wrong time. It would make everything easier…until she fled and they had no idea why. "Really. Go. I'm fine. Wyatt's got to ask me some questions, so he'll be here for a bit." The ability she'd honed as a child, to put on a brave front and act as though the world wasn't exploding, was working to its full effect tonight.

Erin hesitated then glanced at Wyatt, seeming to search for confirmation. Finally, she hugged Jenna, who held on tight for a breath longer than usual. If things went according to plan, she'd be gone by morning and would never again see the closest friend she'd known since her sister's death.

Erin pulled away and turned to Wyatt. "Look out for her."

He tipped his head and walked outside with Jason and Erin, giving Jenna a moment to breathe. She could do this. Half an hour. Make some coffee. Answer some questions. Usher Wyatt out the door.

Then disappear.

One. Two. Three.

Jenna scooped coffee into the filter basket of her coffeepot. Sleep probably wasn't coming any time soon, so caffeine was her friend. The sooner she had a warm mug in her hand, the better she'd feel. Besides, the activity kept her from having to turn toward Wyatt, who stood on the other side of the granite counter.

"Jenna, it's okay to sit still. Nobody's here but us. You're safe."

Four. That's what he thought. "You don't have to stay." Seriously. If he left, she could curl in the corner of her couch and fall apart in peace, grieving what she was about to lose. The fear quaking her insides could run rampant through her body until it subsided.

Then, when the numbness set in, she could save herself.

Reality knifed her chest, causing her breath to hitch. She held the silver spoon tighter, the handle pressing into her palm. Shelley, who owned the building and the coffee shop, had given it to her when she moved in. To-night, she would leave even this small memory behind.

"You said you were making me coffee. I'm going to make sure you keep your promise." There was a rustle as he shifted position. "You might have convinced Erin she didn't have to stay after you gave her the whole it-was-no-big-deal speech, but you're forgetting something. I'm the one who scooped you off the floor like a wet beach towel. You are not okay."

Wow. He had to go and remind her. That kind of ar-rogance was exactly what she expected of Wyatt. To be so smug as to point out her weakness and his strength. The strength she'd felt in his chest through the thick layers of his heavy uniform jacket. For a moment, she'd wanted to stay there. For a moment, she'd felt safe.

Jenna nearly rolled her eyes. Safe with Wyatt Ste-phens? Whether it was her issue or his, they couldn't manage to get along.

The spoon dug into the coffee again, releasing the comforting, earthy aroma of roasted beans, but she hes-itated as she held it over the filter basket. What num-ber was she on?

"That's five." Wyatt's voice was at her shoulder, and he reached around, gently taking the silver spoon from her fingers. His warmth loosened the tension in her shoulders, made her stop feeling like someone was peek-ing through the blinds of her second-story apartment. "Sit. You're wobbling on your feet. I'll finish here."

Normally, when it came to Wyatt she'd argue, but the gelatin in place of her kneecaps was having none of it. Without lifting her head, Jenna sidestepped him and walked around the column at the end of the bar into the small living room at the front of the apartment. She curled into the corner of her gray couch and stared at the picture above the small stone fireplace, the one Erin had painted for her Christmas present. It was an almost photographic recreation of the view from Anson's Ridge. When the days were rough or the memories too real, Jenna escaped up there to be alone. She'd head that way right now if rain wasn't moving in.

And if she wasn't more afraid than usual of what might lurk in the dark.

She'd probably never see Anson's Ridge again. Her eyes burned, tears pushing to the front. Leaving El Paso had been hard, but with nothing to keep her there, her departure hadn't ripped her heart into pieces.

This time, leaving might kill her.

Dragging her hands through her hair, she stared at the painting and wished herself into it.

A heavy pottery mug appeared in her vision, steam curling above it.

Jenna jumped, her hand over her heart. She'd have to relearn how to be vigilant.

"Sorry." With an apologetic smile that looked well practiced, Wyatt backed away, still holding the mug out to her. "Didn't mean to scare you. I found creamer in the fridge and assumed you'd want it in your coffee."

His blue eyes were a startling contrast to his dark hair. She'd never noticed before, likely because she'd never been this close before. Then again, maybe without all of the tension that usually flowed between them, she could see him more clearly.

His eyes were actually kind of nice.

He held the cup a little closer, his cheeks reddening as though he could read her thoughts. "You want it or not?"

"Sorry." Jenna wrapped both hands around the mug, careful not to brush his fingers. They'd been close enough to each other for one night already, and now she was noticing his eyes? *No bueno.* "Thanks." The warmth from the ceramic seeped into her fingers, inched its way up her arms and settled into her soul. Finally, she could relax, even if it was all a temporary illusion of peace.

Before her sister, Amy, died, she had gone to a therapist and had doled out advice she received there. *Best way to get rid of the ugly is to focus on the right now,* Amy's therapist had said. *The whole Matthew 6 thing about tomorrow having its own troubles means you should focus now.* Funny how her sister's secondhand wisdom popped to mind tonight.

Jenna could focus on *right now*, on the familiar comforting warmth of a mug in her hands. On the creamy walls she'd painted with Erin when she'd first rented the apartment.

On the police officer whose presence seemed way too big for the tiny space of her living room.

Hands practically engulfing his own sapphire-blue mug, Wyatt sat in an armchair in the corner near the window and stared into his coffee. He didn't move until his radio crackled. He listened, then spoke into the mic at his shoulder, ending with "Ten six."

"What are those numbers?" The numbers were eas-

ier to talk about than any questions he'd have for her.
"'Ten six?'"

"Means I'm busy unless it's urgent. I'm in the middle
of something and can't be interrupted unless the world's
about to explode."

He was trying to be funny, but nothing about it was
amusing. She was the most important thing on a police
officer's agenda.

Wyatt took a sip of coffee, then inspected the mug.
"This is nice. Well made. The color's rich. You buy them
from someone around here?" He lifted the crafted piece
to look for a mark on the bottom.

He wouldn't find one. Jenna had made them herself,
but she couldn't say so. No one around town knew she
threw pottery, that she'd done so since she'd learned
in one of the after-school programs in El Paso. She
took pleasure in the wet clay as she infused beauty
into something unbelievably plain, like Jesus had done
with her.

She'd love to share her work, but it was one of the
things she'd had to keep in the dark, packed away to
protect her safety.

Of course, none of her caution mattered now.

The room took on the kind of awkward silence that
made the air heavier, as though a black hole spun over
the sleek glass coffee table. All she wanted was to be
alone, yet Wyatt sat and sipped his coffee, acting like
this was some sort of extended social call.

Of course, she'd been the one to tell him he could
have coffee, but only because he'd probably saved her
life, then made sure her apartment was safe. It would

have been kind of rude to kick him out after he'd been on the front lines for her.

Oh, man. He'd been in every room of her apartment. There had better not be any dirty laundry in the middle of the bedroom floor. Her cheeks heated. "You don't have to stay."

He met her gaze and held it. "I don't have a choice."

"Erin said you had to? Was that your conversation outside when she left?" Jenna's best friend was the only female firefighter on the Mountain Springs Volunteer Fire Department. She had been the protective type even before she'd almost fallen victim to a serial killer. "You know Erin's not your boss. You don't have to do what she says."

Wyatt's laugh was quick and seemed to come from deep in his chest. In other circumstances, his mirth might have lifted her spirits. "You know you're living in a fantasy world, right? Erin's all about taking charge. It's a good possibility if I don't obey her commands, I'll never hear the end of it. It's easier to nod and agree, especially while she's living in my house." His smile slipped and the serious expression that usually resided on his face took over. "This time it's my real boss who's calling the shots."

Jenna leaned forward and set her coffee mug on the table. "What?"

"As long as the guy who tried to take you is out there, I'm supposed to keep an eye on you, at least for the short term. Plus, I still have to take your statement."

"So I'm your assignment?"

"If you want to use those words, sure."

"And you have to stay in my home for the foresee-able future?" His constant presence was going to put a definite crimp in her plans.

But maybe…

Maybe there was hope. It fluttered in her chest, dar-ing her to reach out and grasp it.

If Wyatt was watching out for her, she wouldn't have to leave. Maybe they'd catch whoever the man was be-fore he could try again.

"I won't crash in your apartment. I'll be in my vehi-cle." Wyatt shifted and sat on the edge of his seat, hold-ing his coffee mug between his knees. "Do you know who the man was?"

"I've never seen him before." Technically, it was true. She'd never seen that particular man in her life. She'd have remembered the dark eyes, the scar along his cheek. But she'd known plenty of men like him.

Jenna was hiding from one.

Logan had been handsome. Charming… Until he had her under his thumb and threw the first punch. She could still feel the shock of it—physically and mentally. Her lower jaw tightened. Her lip trembled. She dug her teeth in and reached for her mug, but her hand shook, and she sloshed coffee onto the glass.

Wyatt pulled in a deep breath, watching her with a prac-ticed gaze before he spoke. "What are you not telling me?"

"Nothing." She should probably confess, but what good would it do? If there was even the slimmest chance she could preserve her new identity and stay in town, the last thing she needed to do was bust everything into the open.

Wyatt stood, then stalked to the kitchen and set his

mug on the bar with a thump, making Jenna jump. "This?" He turned toward her, familiar suspicion in his eyes, making the blue turn granite gray. "This is my problem. This is what frustrates me about you."

Her head jerked back so hard her neck strained. "What?" She stood and squared off with him, the fear from her earlier encounter finding new fire in her anger. "What exactly are you accusing me of? A man broke in to my shop tonight. Am I suddenly the bad guy?"

Wyatt dragged his hand down his face and along the back of his neck, where he dug his fingers in. "No, but you're definitely not telling me the truth."

"I don't know who the guy was, okay?"

"Fine. Then answer this… Was it a robbery gone wrong? A kidnapping attempt?" Straightening, Wyatt crossed his arms. "You may not know who he was, but do you have any clue why he was there? Give me something to work with, Jenna."

Wait a second. Jenna backed away, her eyebrows inching closer to her hairline. Something didn't make sense. For all Wyatt knew, he'd foiled a simple break-in, one where Jenna was merely caught in the middle. He didn't know the real story, had no idea she'd been targeted. Yet the bodyguard duty, the intensity and direction of his questions…

It seemed as though he did.

Her jaw slackened and she swallowed hard. Maybe Wyatt Stephens had a problem with her all of these years because he knew the one thing she'd tried the hardest to hide.

Exactly who she really was.

THREE

I can't give you anything. Wyatt dropped his head against the seat of his truck and stared across the street at Jenna's apartment. Maybe he was being overly suspicious, but it sure did feel like her insistence was a lie. Fine. He'd go around her. He'd find out the truth on his own.

Any news yet? Wyatt tapped out the message to fellow officer Brian Early, then rested his cell phone on his leg, settling in his seat to watch Jenna's front door. He'd had Early bring his personal truck then take his SUV to the station. He wanted to remain as inconspicuous as possible as he sat parked in the dark end of the alley across the street from Jenna's apartment. Thankfully, the historic building's second story offered only one way in, the very stairs he'd practically had to chase her up earlier to keep her from running headlong into the unknown of her own apartment.

In some ways, she appeared to be heedless of the danger. In others, she appeared to be hyperaware of exactly what was going on, of what his department suspected. A brazen attack on Jenna could be random, or it could mean traffickers had already gained a toehold in the town, and they weren't planning to be too careful about hiding themselves. If that was the case, this could be the start of a violent struggle for control of his hometown.

It was a leap, sure, to go from an attack on one woman to a human trafficking ring that had been dormant since the early fall. But his gut... His gut wouldn't let him downplay the coincidence of those Texas license plates. A thin thread, but a thread nonetheless.

His phone buzzed on his thigh and he glanced at the screen. Nothing yet. Guy's a ghost. Could be he cut and ran.

Anything on the car? They'd called in the county and had the car behind Jenna's shop processed, but it would take time to get more than an owner's name. Without a clear link to the traffickers, nobody higher up the chain than the county was going to get involved. In fact, the state and federal agents had cleared out weeks ago, their final report stating the gang had either had trouble with the van while passing through, or had been spooked enough by law enforcement's presence to move on.

The almost-physical gnawing at the back of Wyatt's brain said no.

His phone buzzed. Registered in Texas. Same county as the box truck. Working on getting more.

Thanks. Pushing deeper into his seat, Wyatt worked his shoulders back and forth, trying to ease some of the tension building there. Jenna had been cagey tonight. She tended to keep a low profile, and she was definitely hiding something. She'd asserted a dozen times that she didn't know the man who'd been waiting for her in the shop, and Wyatt had finally stopped asking.

But something about her answers to his questions rang false. No, he didn't think she was a criminal, but she certainly was not telling him the truth. *Frustrating* would be an understatement.

Chief Thompson was going to have to put someone else on this protection detail. Even with thin evidence, the man was cautious, wanting to be certain the smugglers weren't behind this. Mountain Springs wasn't a town with a high crime rate, even with all of the tourist activity. Violent crime was practically nonexistent. A kidnapping was unheard of.

The suspect was definitely an outsider, and no one randomly came to town to cause trouble. Until they knew for certain Jenna was safe, they'd keep an eye on her. But Wyatt couldn't be the guy on point this time. The two of them had the worst kind of personality conflict. Worse than oil and water, they were ammonia and bleach. Put them in the same room and everyone else fled to get away from the toxic reaction.

And that was on a normal day, when she had no reason to lie.

Wyatt had had his fill of lying women. After what Kari had done to him, it was hard enough to trust anyone else. Nearly a decade later, the wound his former fiancée had inflicted still smarted, mostly in his pride. She'd strung him along for months, her eyes on what she viewed as "the prize." Wyatt had been a young soldier from a small town, ignorant of the fact there were women in the world who preyed on guys like him, on the steady paycheck and benefits the army offered.

Hearing Kari tell a friend on the eve of their wedding how she'd "hit the jackpot" in death benefits and insurance if he died while deployed...

Her callousness had gutted him. The calculated way her expression shifted from disdain to adoration when he made himself known and it was clear what he'd heard... She'd tried to play it off as the nervousness of a young bride, as a joke.

His life was no joke.

His heart hadn't shattered when he'd turned and walked out of the room, away from his dreams for the future. It had hardened into a mountain of stone.

Jenna Clark's behavior since she'd arrived in town shook that mountain like an earthquake every time he looked at her. Something about her had a way of tweaking his attitude.

Leaning forward, he studied the front of the building that housed Higher Grounds Coffee Bar downstairs and Jenna's apartment upstairs. Lights still shone from the coffee shop, which had stayed open past its usual eleven o'clock closing time due to the shows at the Fine Arts Center. Couples and groups of all ages flowed in and out of the large glass front door, seeking warmth against the cold, likely too full of energy from the bluegrass concert to head to the bed-and-breakfasts in town or the hotels about half an hour away. Nobody seemed out of place or overly interested in Jenna's apartment upstairs.

He leaned forward an inch more. Light poured from the upstairs windows. If he'd expected Jenna to make her way to bed and at least try to rest by now, he'd have missed the mark. She probably wouldn't catch five minutes of sleep tonight.

Leaving her alone had felt wrong, as though he had abandoned her, but he couldn't stay after she'd turned on him and practically threw him out. Wyatt's question had hit a nerve, but as much as he'd replayed their conversation before she showed him the door, he couldn't figure out what was wrong.

Unless, though she'd denied it repeatedly, she truly knew the man who'd had his arm wrapped around her throat.

In the big picture, did it matter? The image of Jenna being treated so roughly made him bristle with anger and dredged up memories he fought daily to keep buried. Nobody did that to a woman.

Nobody.

A crowd of seven or eight college students exited the coffee shop and made a right up the hill toward the Fine Arts Center and the parking lot beyond it. A man at the rear of the pack broke away and edged to the left. He wore a hat pulled low so that his face was hidden in shadow. He leaned against the faded brick at the end of the building closest to Jenna's, seeming disinterested in the crowd. The way his head moved, though, he was watching. Waiting.

Wyatt sat taller and wrapped his fingers around the door handle. The guy could have a buddy inside paying their bill. He could be two seconds from lighting a cigarette.

Or he could be trouble.

After double-checking to make sure the interior lights in the truck were off, Wyatt slipped out and eased the door shut.

The stranger didn't seem to notice. He simply stood, leaning against the wall, watching as a chatting, laughing group passed between his position and Wyatt's.

When the people cleared the space, the man lifted his head and looked directly across the street at Wyatt. With a sly half smile, the man lifted his hand and flicked a two-fingered mocking salute against his forehead before he turned toward the stairs to Jenna's apartment.

A jolt of familiarity shot through Wyatt. He was the same man who'd tried to kidnap Jenna at her shop. Wyatt shifted to run, but a weight slammed into the small of his back, driving him to the ground and forcing the breath from his lungs. His cheek smacked the pavement and he slid several inches on his chest, rough gravel grinding into his shoulder. Using the momentum from the fall, he rolled onto his back and threw his arm out in time to deflect a blow from a muscular man wearing a dark shirt and a baseball cap.

His face wasn't covered, which could only mean one thing…

He didn't intend to let Wyatt live long enough to identify him.

With a lethal smile, he dove toward Wyatt, his face shadowed in the dim light from across the street.

Wyatt rolled to the side, years of military and police training kicking in with a vicious muscle memory. As his attacker stumbled, Wyatt threw out his leg and kicked beneath the left knee.

The man went to the ground with a howl, his cheek smacking the pavement with a sickening thud.

Handcuffs out before he even thought to grab them, Wyatt planted a knee in the man's back and held him to the ground, cuffing his attacker before he could catch his breath. Tugging a second pair of cuffs from his belt, Wyatt jerked the guy upward and anchored him to the tow hook on the truck bumper.

The stranger's head lolled to the side, blood dripping from his top lip, where his teeth had driven in. He sneered at Wyatt with a horrid amusement. "Don't be in any hurry. The girl's already dead."

Footsteps pounded on the metal stairs outside the apartment.

Jenna set the coffeepot on the granite kitchen counter next to the .38 revolver she'd taken out of her closet after Wyatt left. The likelihood she would be able to pull the trigger while aiming at another human being was almost zero, but it still made her feel better to have protection at hand.

She stared over the bar at the door as the footsteps stopped outside. Wyatt had probably decided he had more intrusive questions to ask. Well, the door was dead bolted and the chain was on. Let him think she'd gone to sleep, was in the shower, whatever… He was not coming in here again tonight. She had to have time to think, to pray. The packed bag in the attic called to her, but what if running wasn't the way out this time?

The door rattled as he grabbed the knob, then there was silence.

Jenna reached for the coffee carafe again.

The door exploded inward, wood splintering around the lock.

The coffeepot slipped from Jenna's hands, hit the side of the sink and shattered in the basin as she released a strangled cry and stumbled backward until her back collided with the cold stainless steel refrigerator.

A man hulked in her doorway.

Not *a* man. *The* man. The one from her shop. The same leer curled his lip as he stepped onto her door and stood between her table and her couch, blocking her exit.

Panic robbed her muscles of strength. She couldn't breathe, couldn't think, couldn't move. There was nothing to do but stare as the man stalked slowly toward her, his dark eyes never leaving hers. A deepening bruise ran along his jaw where Wyatt had delivered a near-crippling blow earlier.

Wyatt. He was watching. He had to have seen what was happening. He'd be on the stairs any second, bursting through the door to save her. She swallowed hard, pulled herself taller and found her voice. "You'd better leave. The police are watching."

"Is that a fact?" The man stopped, his chuckle a low rumble. "You mean your boyfriend? The hero who rescued you earlier?" He sniffed and waved a hand in the direction of the door, his eyes practically glittering with amusement. "Sorry, hon. By now, he's dead."

The words hit her in the chest, rocking her backward until she was pressed fully against the refrigerator. The cold of the metal seeped through her shirt into her spine, bringing a shiver. No. He had to be lying. Wyatt couldn't be dead because of her.

He couldn't be dead at all.

Methodically, as though he enjoyed torturing her with his presence, the man stepped closer until he stood in the doorway of the kitchen between the column and the wall, a few feet from her position. "Here's what you need to know to make this easier on both of us." His hand went to his side and rested at his hip, where a gun was likely concealed beneath his navy blue windbreaker. "My boss pays me whether I bring you in alive or dead, though there's twice as much in the bank if you're breathing. He'd like the pleasure of taking care of you himself. It's really up to you to decide what happens next. You can come to Texas with me all nice and quiet, or you can find yourself in the morgue next to your boyfriend. Either way, my wallet thanks you."

The truth hardened her resolve and it flowed from her core to strengthen her weakened joints. If she walked meekly out her front door with this man and let him take her to El Paso, she was dead. Logan would never let her survive, not if he was willing to go to these lengths to drag her to her past.

No. She could die right here, but at least she'd go down fighting. She turned and backed down the long galley kitchen one foot, two. If she could reach a knife, something…

Her gaze drifted to the counter. The pistol.

His eyes followed hers and he walked into the kitchen, feet heavy on the tile floor. "I wouldn't if I were you. You'll never make it."

No, she wouldn't. Jenna jerked her hand toward the gun and, when the man lunged for it, she shifted to the right and shoved his back with everything she had in her, edging around him as he stumbled off balance and crashed into the wall behind her.

She ran for the door as more footsteps rang on the stairs from outside. Jenna stopped, her heart thumping painfully, freedom a breath away.

She was trapped.

A man appeared in the doorway.

Wyatt, his pistol drawn. In one smooth motion, he grabbed her by the wrist and tugged her behind him, leveling his weapon on the assailant in her kitchen. The man grabbed his head and stood staring wide-eyed at the police officer he'd assumed was dead.

"Put your hands behind your head. Don't you dare even twitch in any other direction." Wyatt's voice was deep and commanding, daring the stranger to disobey him.

More sounds on the stairs. Officers Brian Early and Mike Owens crowded around Wyatt, weapons drawn, easing into the room.

Holstering his pistol as the other officers moved to apprehend their suspect, Wyatt reached for Jenna and drew her to his chest, resting his cheek on the top of her head.

"It's over. We got him."

Jenna shook her head. He could believe it was over if he wanted, but it wasn't. There was clearly a price on her head, and unless Logan lifted the bounty…she was dead.

FOUR

"It's time to tell the truth." Wyatt held a glass out to Jenna. She was huddled in the corner of the couch, staring at the door that Greg Jenkins from the hardware store had hastily repaired. Apparently, Wyatt had sent out a late-night emergency plea to the Summit Community Church men's group.

Wyatt's actions were déjà vu, but this time he handed her water instead of coffee. And this time, instead of taking a seat across the room, he settled onto the end of the sofa, his boots planted on the hardwood, his elbows resting on his knees. Deep scrapes marred his cheek, and he stared at Jenna with a bizarre blend of frustration and pity.

Setting the water on the coffee table, Jenna stared at her hands. It was nearly two in the morning, a time when her brain surrendered to exhaustion and sheened the world with a nightmarish tint.

Her worst fears unfolded before her eyes in the most heinous of ways, and now she had to contend with the man who was the definition of "personality conflict" carefully watching her every move.

Nothing felt real, not even Wyatt's presence. He was so close she could reach across the couch and poke him in the arm, or press her forehead into his shoulder the way she had earlier. He'd stood in the middle of her living room and held her while his fellow officers escorted that terrifying man out of her home. Had held her while another returned to report they'd taken the man who'd attacked Wyatt into custody. He'd held her until the shaking fear began and didn't let go until her trembling ended in numb, cavernous calm.

Jenna didn't know what to do with feeling safe in his arms—it was a reaction she'd never expected. It made no sense he should care. She meant nothing to him, yet she couldn't calculate how long Wyatt had stood holding her against his chest, occasionally telling her everything was okay and she was safe.

"I'm not safe." The words slipped out, a whisper that brought immediate regret. What she wouldn't give for a way to inhale them right into her lungs.

She tensed, waiting. Maybe they'd been too low for Wyatt to hear.

The way his shoulders stiffened said otherwise. He angled toward her, though his feet stayed planted in front of him. For a long time, he watched her as though trying to read her secrets, then he abruptly turned toward the fireplace. "You have to tell me everything. If you're in danger, I need to know why."

"You don't know already?"

"If I did, would I ask?"

Jenna opened her mouth, then dug her teeth into her bottom lip. She'd spent three years burying Genevieve

Brady, careful not to say or do anything that could lead Logan to her. She'd laughed at her fear on occasion, at the idea of Logan caring enough to search for her, let alone possessing the ability to find her in tiny Mountain Springs. Still, she'd never believed in taking chances. Now her caution proved wise, yet futile.

"Jenna." Wyatt's impatience leaked into his voice in a tone she knew well.

The time for hiding was over. There was no other way to protect herself or those she loved. "I'm…" The truth refused to budge. The lock was too rusty, the fear too real.

Maybe if she started at the beginning, the small truths would loosen the bonds around the bigger ones. "I didn't have a childhood like yours, a mom and a dad who loved me." She sniffed and waved her hand as though it encompassed the world. "I don't even know who my father is. It's right on my birth certificate, a screaming white space where his name should be." The shame burned. She was, and always would be, the girl without a father, the product of… What? Of love? Of hate? Of pain?

Wyatt's eyebrows drew together, almost as though he couldn't comprehend. "You know nothing about him?"

"Nothing. Not his hair color, his age, if he's dead or alive…" Jenna grabbed the throw pillow from where she'd dropped it on the floor and held it to her chest, toying with the fringe. "I don't know if my mother never knew who he was or if she hated him or…what. She never talked about him, and the few times Amy or I asked, she changed the subject."

"Amy's your sister?"

"My twin sister. She died in a car accident three years ago."

"I'm sorry."

Not as sorry as Jenna was. She should have been there for Amy. In a perfect world, she would have been. "We were almost identical, except she's blond and I'm caught somewhere between brown and red." The burgundy pillow fringe knotted beneath her fingers, but Jenna couldn't make herself care. She'd never spoken about her childhood to anyone except her twin sister. They had suffered under a mother who loved herself more than her children. The story was unfamiliar on her tongue, nearly impossible to put into words. "My mom lived in this someday-my-prince-will-come fantasy. She was constantly looking for the perfect man. She relationship hopped. Sometimes she brought them home, sometimes she took off with them." Through it all, Constance Brady had ignored her daughters and left them to fend for themselves, only concerned with her own happiness. How often had she abandoned them for weeks to run off with a man she'd eventually dropped?

Wyatt's expression shifted to wary compassion. He held a hand out to Jenna, then let it rest on the couch between them. "Did they hurt you?"

"No. Never. Most of them she ran off with and we never saw. The ones who bothered to come around the apartment were usually somehow the good ones. She was this fragile, almost ethereal woman. Men had this thing about wanting to protect her. She wasn't the stereotypical bad-boy magnet. It's hard to believe, I know." It was actually impossible to believe, but all of her mother's boyfriends had essentially doted on her and ignored Jenna and Amy.

"My mother loved the newness, the fairy tale, the falling in love. Once it got hard, she was done." Until Anthony. He'd stayed longer than any other boyfriend, had treated them like a family…for a while. "The last one she stayed with for almost two years. He was different. He literally wouldn't let her edge him out. He truly cared about me and Amy, maybe more than our mother."

A chunk of the fringe rolled off in her fingers. Jenna dropped it onto the table. The night she'd fled, Anthony had appeared in her semidark hospital room. It was the first time he'd made contact in years. His hair was grayer, his brown eyes bracketed by deep lines. He'd held her hand in the same fatherly way he'd always had. "Your mom tried so many times to kick me out. Fact was, I knew she never cared about me past how I made her feel. But you girls needed a father figure. You were getting to the age where you needed someone to look out for you and I—I couldn't have kids. You were like my own. I never should've let her kick me to the curb but she was right to do it. My work…"

He'd stopped talking, but Jenna knew. His work was likely putting them in danger. He had never been legit. He was tied to things she could never know about, was by his own admission well-known for helping anyone— from wanted criminals to terrified underlings—start over anywhere in the world. Anthony was a master of forged documents and false stories.

His criminal talents had saved her life.

The pillow shifted and Jenna jumped, slammed into the reality of her living room. She was once again facing a life on the run from a man who either wanted to possess her or wanted her dead.

Wyatt took the pillow from her hands and laid it out of reach on the coffee table. "You're torturing an innocent piece of interior decorating. I can't sit by and watch."

Jenna laughed. It felt good. Right... For a second. "Not long after Anthony left, my mom killed herself. Swallowed a bunch of sleeping pills. Amy and I were sixteen. Long story, but we petitioned for emancipation and won."

It had almost been easier without their mother. They'd been taking care of themselves for years, going to school and working. As time passed, Amy took a personal training gig at New Horizons Day Spa. Jenna built her following in the local art world.

"You think this guy your mother dated is the one who's after you?" Reaching for his phone, Wyatt poised his finger over the screen to take notes. "What's his name? Where's—"

"No." Jenna put her hand on Wyatt's wrist. It was warm beneath her fingers, tensed for action.

Tensed to protect her.

It made no sense.

She jerked her hand away and placed it in her lap, fiddling with the hem of her shirt. "Anthony helped me get out of El Paso and start a life here. I think the man who's after me is..." She hadn't uttered his name aloud since the night she fled forever. It stuck like a razor blade in her throat. "Logan Cutter."

Wyatt typed something into his phone, likely a text

to someone at the station so they could start digging. "Who is he?"

"My ex-boyfriend. Before I became a Christian." Aside from guilt at having cut Amy from her life, Jenna's relationship with Logan was the shame she bore. She'd run straight off the rails on their second date. "I promised myself I'd never be like my mother. I'd never go looking for Prince Charming, but Logan was. He sold and maintained equipment at the gym where Amy worked. He was about eight years older than me, had money to throw around, took care of me. Made me feel like…" Jenna buried her head in the couch cushion. She didn't want to talk about this, especially not to a guy as straitlaced as Wyatt.

He slipped his hand between the cushion and her cheek and gently lifted her head. "You never had a father in your life. You were looking for someone to give you security, to love you unconditionally, the kinds of things a father does for his daughter… Or a man does for the woman he loves." Wyatt's voice weighed heavy, as though he could see inside her heart. "What did he do to you?"

"He isolated me from everyone, even Amy. For several years, I turned my back on every relationship for him. I figured when he was jealous, it was because he wanted to be with me. But he was never faithful even when I was living under his roof. He was…" The hard part. The part Amy had uncovered and tried to warn her about. The part that still made her plant both feet on the floor in case she had to outrun the nausea. "He was trafficking women. And when I found out and tried to leave him…"

The first time, he'd denied his depravity and slapped her, then apologized. Held her. Lavished her with gifts. The second time he'd hit her more than once. And the third? She couldn't remember much of the third after he slammed her head into the wall.

"I thought I was safe here, but… I have to leave."

"Not this time." Wyatt's voice was deep, husky in a way that sent a warm shiver from the inside out. His fingers, strong and reassuring, wrapped around Jenna's, but he didn't move closer. He didn't need to. "You were alone in El Paso, isolated from your friends, without any family. This time's different. You have an entire town behind you. Before you run all alone, let somebody protect you. Let us end this for good."

Jenna let her hand linger in his before she pulled away. She might not be alone, but trusting Wyatt could set her free…or get her killed.

A door clicked shut and Wyatt was instantly on his feet, scanning his surroundings. He reached for the gun he'd rested close by after Jenna went to bed in the dark hours of the morning. Twice he'd had to rescue her from men intent on taking her away.

He couldn't let it happen again.

The small apartment was still. The security bar he'd placed beneath the doorknob before he grabbed some sleep was still wedged to the floor. Dim light from streetlamps pooled meekly through the blinds onto the dark hardwood.

From somewhere deep in the apartment came the sound of running water. Jenna must be awake.

Wyatt glanced at his watch. Not quite five. Had she slept? After telling him her story, she'd seemed spent, and he'd sent her to rest. He'd done some cursory research on his laptop and reported in, setting into motion the means of tracking down Logan Cutter. He couldn't access much from his machine, but it hadn't taken much of a database search to piece together the truth in Jenna's story. Cutter's company had abruptly shut the doors two years prior due to tax issues. Court records had been sealed, which was something worth looking into, but the man hadn't done any prison time. No "Logan Cutter" appeared on an inmate search.

Still, Logan's past was enough to make Wyatt even more suspicious of the link between the panel truck on Overton Road and the attacks on Jenna. While Wyatt believed Jenna was telling the truth about her relationship with Logan, she was still hiding something. There had been too many gaps in her story. The best thing to do was to keep her close, to gain her trust and pray she eventually spilled something to let the authorities stop men like Logan Cutter from taking up a strategic position in Mountain Springs.

He'd run a quick search on Jenna, too. Her name hadn't raised any red flags on the databases he had access to. In order to search deeper, he'd have to go through the department's system. He wasn't sure he wanted to. While he knew she was holding back, he wasn't sure he wanted to find out how much.

Sitting back on the couch, he ran his tongue over his teeth. He felt every bit like he'd slept in his clothes last night. Too hot, grimy from head to toe. At some point, he'd have to hand Jenna over to another officer so he could run home and grab a shower, but he wouldn't stay gone long. No way was he going off duty at nine as scheduled. Whether they paid him overtime or not, he was sticking close to Jenna Clark.

Despite her hiding something, he'd developed a grudging admiration for her and a white-hot anger at any man who'd treat a woman the way she'd been treated. Domestic abuse was his hot button, ever since his first call as a rookie cop. His army deployments had shown him the worst of mankind, but he'd never expected to encounter the level of violence on the home front as he'd encountered on a fateful August day a few years earlier.

Julia Pritchett had made a frantic phone call to 911 when her husband, Chad, flew at her in his latest drunken rage. By the time Wyatt and other officers on duty arrived, Chad was already firing out the window, determined to go down shooting.

The bullet that grazed Wyatt's shoulder had sent a burning shock through him. He'd made it through two deployments unscathed only to get hit at home. Mind racing, fear pumping, he'd watched the situation spiral out of control, had been powerless to do anything but take cover with the other officers, to wait for help to come from the county…

To listen helplessly as Chad pulled the trigger two final times, ending Julia's life and his own.

Those deaths had nearly broken Wyatt, had sent his mind spiraling through a series of what-ifs. What if the bullet had been a few small inches to the left? What if

Julia had pressed charges sooner? What if Wyatt had been brave enough to storm the house and neutralize the threat before it was too late?

He'd given the guilt to God, forgiven himself and even Chad, but he carried one very important lesson from those events... Never, ever lose control of the situation.

He prayed daily for God to protect his family and the people of Mountain Springs, and then Wyatt suited up and went out to be the hands and feet to do the work.

Meanwhile, half a continent away, Jenna Clark had been facing her own nightmare.

Respect dulled the edge of his wariness. While the lawman in him couldn't necessarily approve of her methods, it had taken a special kind of courage for her to leave everything and start over where she knew no one and had nothing. From the outside, she'd built a decent living at The Color Café, though she was by no means rich.

He glanced around the apartment. Shelley Nelson, who owned the historic building, had done some updates before Jenna came to town, but the sleek paint and the polished hardwood were all Jenna's time and muscle. Well, Jenna's and Erin's. She'd even managed to make the hodgepodge of furniture Shelley had gathered look as though it was meant to be a collection. Slightly artsy and a little bit funky, the space was much like the woman who called it home.

"Want some coffee?"

Jumping to his feet, Wyatt turned and found Jenna standing at the end of the bar. He hadn't even heard her approach.

She'd towel dried her auburn hair and it hung in waves, barely skimming the shoulders of her loose purple sweater. Padding around in blue jeans and bare feet with her face scrubbed free of makeup, she almost looked like a lost teenager.

A fierce protectiveness surged. He'd made her a promise last night, a promise to catch Logan Cutter and set her free. He was more determined than ever to keep it.

The ferocity of the emotion caught Wyatt off guard. He cleared his throat. She was waiting for an answer to a question he'd nearly forgotten. *Oh, wait...* "Coffee? You don't have a pot." He'd spent the first few minutes after she went to bed picking glass out of her kitchen sink so she wouldn't have to see the reminder.

Jenna's expression clouded, then she lifted a sheepish shrug. "Always have a spare coffee maker, Stephens. Makes life more livable."

When she turned and walked into the kitchen, Wyatt followed and took a seat on a bar stool across the counter from her. "What is it with you and coffee? It was your first instinct last night and again this morning."

She didn't turn, simply reached beneath the counter, pulled out what looked to be an older inexpensive coffee maker and plugged it in next to the stove. "Coffee's cheap."

"Okay..."

"When I was a kid and my mother would take off, there wasn't a lot of food in the house. She never got around to applying for any kind of aid. We lived on PB and J and white bread and milk. There was no money for splurging on treats, but coffee and sugar and milk go a long way. So if it was a rough night or I was more upset than usual, Amy would make coffee, load it full of milk and sugar, and we'd sit in the den and pretend we were all grown, in college, hanging at the coffee shop." Jenna paused with the coffee bag in her hands and stared at the contents, then inhaled deeply. "She had a way of making the hard times more like a game. So now…" She shrugged again and started scooping coffee into the filter.

So now it was her way of feeling closer to her sister, of comforting herself. "Kind of ironic God gave you a business where you can sell coffee *and* found you an apartment over a coffee shop, huh?"

She chuckled and pressed the button on the coffee maker before she turned to him. "It always smells really good in here, if you hadn't noticed."

He had. The scent of brewing coffee permeated the apartment, both from Jenna's machine and the larger ones downstairs as well.

"You mentioned God." Jenna sighed and leaned against the counter, crossing her arms over her chest. "I've trusted Him the past three years, ever since Erin walked in on day one and started helping me paint the shop. I didn't even know her. She walked into the building and jumped right in, started talking about Jesus, and it made sense. Thing is…" Her green eyes, hazy and troubled, met his. "He didn't answer my prayers, did He? He didn't keep me safe."

Her doubt prickled along Wyatt's spine. He couldn't let her lose faith because of a man like Logan. "His not operating in exactly the way you expect Him to doesn't mean He doesn't care."

"Maybe." Jenna turned and grabbed two blue pottery mugs from the cabinet, then set them onto the counter with a *thunk* that signaled some sort of finality. "But it does mean my trust might have been misplaced."

Wyatt opened his mouth to argue, but his phone buzzed on the coffee table. He hesitated, not wanting to leave her with her misconceptions, but being alert to the dangers of the real world took precedence.

Reluctantly, he slipped from the stool and crossed the room to retrieve his phone.

"How is Jenna this morning?" Chief Thompson's voice was all business.

Wyatt glanced over his shoulder to where Jenna was pouring creamer into a mug. He stepped toward the window, out of sight around the edge of the hallway, and lowered his voice. "Still a little shaken. I want to stay with her today." He braced himself for the answer. Arch Thompson was all about protocol, and making sure Wyatt was rested was part of the protocol.

"You know, I wasn't kidding when I said I wanted somebody with her 24/7 until we get to the bottom of what's going on here. With the information you sent over this morning, I'm even more concerned than ever with finding out what she knows and with keeping her out of harm's way until she can tell us, but you have to rest at some point."

"I slept after I sent the info to you this morning."

"It couldn't have been more than a couple of hours." Chief Thompson made a clicking sound with his tongue.

"I'll send Hayes over in a few minutes so you can go home and get cleaned up. Early took a couple of hours of leave this morning. Nina's sick."

That made sense. Early would do anything for his sister. "I hope she's okay." Nina Early was a sophomore at Appalachian State. Their parents had been killed in a skiing accident a couple of years earlier, and she was all Brian had left. "I'll check in with him later."

"Do it. And if you promise me you'll find a way to rest, I'll keep you with Jenna. Truth is, with your military experience, I'm a little more comfortable with you taking point on this one anyway." A veteran himself, Arch Thompson knew the rigors of training and combat.

"I'll be safe."

"I know you will." The line was muffled for a second, probably because the chief was shifting hands. He did that a lot—passed the radio or the phone from hand to hand, particularly when he was tense. "I contacted Agent Connor Nance, who headed the investigation last fall, and let him know what's going on. They're sending a small team to sniff around, see if this was an isolated incident or something to worry about. They want to stay low-key, so don't expect a big presence. You may not even see them. Jenna is to go about her normal routine with them watching. They'll steer clear of contacting her, let anybody watching think we're the sole law-enforcement presence in the vicinity. Might make our bad guys get comfortable enough to make a mistake."

Wyatt wasn't a fan of putting Jenna out in the open, but there wasn't a choice. "Got it."

"There's more." The way Chief Thompson's voice

dropped caused Wyatt to stand taller. "I mentioned Logan Cutter to the Feds, asked them about the sealed court records, if they were tracking him."

"And?"

"And the news isn't good."

Wyatt tightened his grip on the phone. Whatever information the Feds had passed on, it was about to make everything much worse.

FIVE

Jenna slid a plate of toast on the counter in front of the stool Wyatt had vacated a few minutes earlier and set the dish of butter and a jar of Liza's homemade fig preserves next to it. Feeding him was the least she could do after he'd slept on her lumpy couch the night before.

Even though her own stomach was too squirrely to handle more than dry toast, eating was necessary. She'd get all swimmy headed if she didn't force herself to eat something soon, and losing her edge was the last thing she needed.

She poured coffee over the creamer in her mug, wrapped her fingers around the ceramic and leaned against the counter, closing her eyes and letting the warmth take her to the past, to a time when life had been a bit less dramatic, though still complicated. It had been a few minutes since the low rise and fall of Wyatt's voice had ceased, but he hadn't returned to the kitchen yet.

Maybe he'd fallen asleep on the couch, since there was no way he'd caught much rest the night before. He'd been going full tilt by the time she went to bed, and she could still hear his laptop keys clicking when she fell asleep close to four.

The light shifted and she cracked open one eye slightly.

Wyatt stood at the bar, staring at the plate she'd set there. "This for me?"

"Thought you might be hungry. Sorry, but toast is all I have. I usually go downstairs and grab a breakfast sandwich from Shelley's, but I figured with everything going on you'd want me to play today low-key, stay out of sight."

Wyatt's jaw shifted as though he was trying to find a hidden message in the toast. Or, as usual, he didn't trust her.

"I promise I'm not trying to poison you. The butter's straight from Starlight Farms, and Liza made the preserves. I added nothing."

"Good to know." He raised his head to look at her, his eyes bearing an unreadable expression projecting something like sadness…or maybe confusion. It was hard to tell. She'd seen a whole lot more emotions out of him in the past nine or so hours than she had in the past three years, so she was still learning to sort them all out.

"What's wrong?" Jenna lowered her mug and held it against her stomach, dread twisting around the few bites of toast she'd managed to choke down. "Is Erin okay? Jason? Liza?"

"Everybody's fine." He looked down at her across the counter and the difference in their height seemed to double. He cut an imposing figure, still in his uniform, still at the ready to defend her from whatever he wasn't saying.

Jenna set her cup onto the counter, wrapped her fingers around the edge of the cool granite counter and hung on tight. "What is it?"

"For starters, the FBI and Homeland Security are involved."

The air left her lungs in a rush. "What?"

"They need you to go in and open the shop today. Everything in your life needs to continue on exactly the same way as it did before last night. You have to act like you think the men we caught are the ones who were after you and you think you're safe."

"Wyatt, are you serious?" She wasn't safe. She'd told him as much the night before. From what the man in her apartment had said, there was money on the table. Anyone in Logan's circle could come hunting for her, especially if the two who'd been after her last night had given out her location.

"I know this is hard." The lines around Wyatt's eyes deepened, almost as though it pained him to say this as much as it pained her to hear it. "Chances are, for the moment, you're out of the woods. If there really is a price out for you, the two men we have in custody would keep your location to themselves for as long as possible. They wouldn't want to get scooped. Think about it. They lose money if word gets out you're here, especially while they're in custody and can't make a move."

Jenna drew her upper lip between her teeth and ran her thumb along the smooth edge of the counter, almost daring to feel relieved. His theory made sense, sort of. "But how did they find me in the first place?"

"I don't know. We're waiting for them to be questioned."

"Okay." She nodded and stared at the badge on his chest. He'd promised to keep her safe. Surely he wouldn't put her in danger on purpose. "So why do I have to open the shop?"

His chest lifted as though he was preparing for battle, and Jenna braced herself. Going out into the open when she was a potential target wasn't the worst thing he was going to say to her this morning. Dread swirled in her stomach. Her whole life had changed three years ago, had taken another twist last night and was about to hit a spiraling loop again, no doubt.

She wanted off this roller coaster.

"The Feds want you to see if you recognize anyone who comes in to the shop. They also want you to keep an eye out on the tourists who are in town as they pass by. You have those huge windows along the front of the shop."

"This isn't about Logan, is it?" Something bigger was going on, something more than a man out to violently take back someone he believed belonged to him.

"It's not."

"That's why the FBI is involved."

"Yes."

Jenna had lived her life facing her problems head-on, tackling them into submission, finding the solution. Now wasn't the time to knuckle under and be passive. Now was the time to fight. She tried to stand taller, but straighten-

ing her spine didn't put her anywhere near eye to eye with
Wyatt Stephens, whose expression spoke of a troubled
determination to bring justice to whatever situation was
unfolding faster than she could process it.

"You said Logan was..." His jaw tightened and jut-
ted forward slightly as though Logan's crimes were too
terrible to utter aloud.

Jenna nodded once. They were too terrible to hear,
too. She'd lived the horror once of finding out what kind
of man she'd handed her life over to. She didn't need to
relive it ever again.

"Logan Cutter wasn't merely a buyer, Jen." He
wouldn't look away from her but held her gaze as
though he understood the news he was about to deliver was going to rock her world.

He didn't have to say it. Jenna's fingers went to her
mouth, pressing against her lips so tightly her teeth
dug in. "No." She was going to be sick. To pass out.
Her body was going to rebel, to do anything other than
absorb what Wyatt was about to tell her about the man
she'd once thought loved her.

Logan was a much more horrifying monster than
even her worst nightmares had imagined. She swallowed hard and dropped her hands to the counter, seeking balance, something to hold her steady against an
onslaught of vicious truth. "What was he doing?"

"His company was a front. All of the 'equipment' he
was moving around Texas was—"

"Was people." She backed away and her knees gave
out, her back resting against the refrigerator as she slid
to the floor and buried her head between her knees.

She'd lived under his roof, eaten his food, shared his life. All of it bought with—with…

Her eyebrows drew together so tightly her head ached. Her eyes and nose burned with tears that wouldn't come. Her ears buzzed.

The soft sound of movement leaked in right before a weight settled onto the floor next to her and Wyatt leaned his shoulder against hers. "I'm sorry."

Logan had lavished her with gifts. Had wooed her by taking her to fancy restaurants and to other places a girl like her had never imagined she'd go. He'd gradually cut everyone else out of her life until he was everything she had, everything she leaned on, everything she trusted. Even beating her wasn't as bad as this. This was… This was beyond human depravity. "I'm so glad I didn't bring anything from him with me." Her voice was hot and muffled against her jeans.

Wyatt said nothing, simply sat beside her, not moving, simply letting her lean against him as she absorbed the weight of her actions in her former life. *Jesus…* Her heart cried one name. Where would she be if He hadn't saved her from herself after she fled Logan's anger? Who would she be if the Savior of the world hadn't bent to the earth for her and made her a completely different person? If she'd never left Logan, she'd still be bound to a man who…

She couldn't even think it.

Jenna straightened, letting her forearms rest on her knees. She fixed her gaze on the cabinet in front of her as Wyatt eased away and mimicked her posture. "Listen, Jenna…"

There was more coming. Why not? It was as though her life was made up of one twist after another. She was a boulder rolling down a mountain, completely out of control, bouncing in a new direction each time an obstacle appeared in her path. "What?"

"There's a task force investigating the ring Logan worked for and they want your help. They want you to open the shop today. They're hoping to find some more answers through you." He pivoted, resting a hand on her foot. "You don't have to. Say the word and we'll move you to—"

"I'll do it." What choice did she really have? Besides, her cooperation might put Logan and the men he worked with away forever, in a place where they couldn't terrorize another woman.

But wait… Her eyebrows drew together. Based on this discussion, the authorities already had a lot of information on him and the group he worked for. Why did they need her? "What are you not telling me?"

"Logan's not the one who's after you." Wyatt's posture stiffened, then he laid a hand on Jenna's shoulder. There was a long, sickening stretch of silence before he spoke. "Jenna… Logan Cutter is dead."

Jenna pressed her spine against the metal door at the rear of the building while Wyatt paced her shop, pistol in hand. Nausea had persisted since Wyatt had delivered the news, and it left her knees weak and her skin hot.

Logan was dead. Murdered in his own home seven months earlier.

She pressed her fist to her mouth. The urge to run

was strong. Her muscles tensed and were ready for the command, and her skin was sheened in hot sweat. It had been at least a year since her last panic attack.

Seemed her streak was about to end.

She glanced at the small bathroom where her attacker had been concealed the night before and forced herself to breathe through her nose. No one was in there now. It had been the first room Wyatt cleared on his sweep.

But someone had been there last night. Someone who knew her name. No one knew that. No one ever would, not even Wyatt and the Mountain Springs Police Department. Anthony's skills were refined enough to build her an entirely new identity, one that would survive a background check. She didn't want to know how he did it, and she intended to protect her new life at all costs. She could never be Genevieve Brady again.

Yet someone knew her secret. Someone who would have been paid handsomely for taking her to Texas, but by whom? If Logan was dead…

If Logan was dead then none of this made sense. If Logan was dead, she should be free to come out of hiding… Except Logan obviously wasn't the only one who was looking for her.

Jenna kept her hand on the doorknob. She had to run. Had to. But from whom was she running?

And where would she go? Nowhere was safe. Outside stood any number of people looking to take her. Inside stood a man whom she had lost the ability to understand.

Inside also likely held a yucky cleanup.

If she focused on the work she wasn't looking forward to, maybe she could get through this without losing her mind. She'd dumped a lot of paint on the counter last night and it had probably dried into a thick crust by now. In addition to the prep work she should have done last night, the spill would need to be cleaned before she could start the day.

Wyatt appeared at the end of the hallway, his pistol no longer in hand. Likely, it was tucked beneath the hem of the forest green Henley he wore loose over his jeans. She'd always thought the man wore a uniform well, despite his prickly personality. This casual Wyatt, though, the one she now knew also possessed a combination of lethal strength and gentle compassion…

Jenna kept her place at the door, unwilling to let those thoughts run all the way to completion. She had enough to deal with without the uncomfortable task of wrapping her head around the reality of the old Wyatt and this entirely new—and definitely improved—version.

"We're clear. You can head to the front and start doing whatever you need to do. Go about your day like normal." He stopped in front of her office door without meeting her eyes, almost as though he could read her mind and didn't want to encourage her wayward thoughts about him. "All I need for you to do is keep an eye on people, see if you recognize anyone. And if I say move, I need you to move without hesitating. Otherwise, greet customers, serve coffee, teach them to paint. Life is normal and the bad guys haven't phased you at all."

"What about Liza?"

"She comes in at one?" He rested a hand on his hip, drumming his waist. "Let everything go on like usual."

How? When she'd eye every stranger who walked into her shop with suspicion, maybe even fear. Even though the man who'd come after her twice the night before was in custody, she still felt as though someone was watching her every move. The thought crawled all over her skin.

Or maybe it was just Wyatt.

With a bracing breath, she pushed away from the door and started up the narrow hallway, shifting to squeeze past Wyatt where he stood in the entrance to her office.

As she passed, he wrapped his fingers lightly around her wrist.

Her breath caught in her throat and she froze, staring straight ahead, through the shop and out to the deserted early morning street beyond.

Wyatt straightened and dropped her arm, but his chest brushed her shoulder before he backed away. "I know this isn't easy. I know you feel like every closed door is a hiding place, like every stranger is a threat. It's okay. But know this, Jenna…" His other hand rested at the small of her back. His voice was like the low rumble of a distant waterfall, washing over her in waves of something that shimmered in her stomach. "I'm here. I'm not going anywhere. And I refuse to let anything happen to you."

The momentary panic that had weakened her joints earlier leaped sideways, replaced by something completely different…though the effect was exactly the same. Nodding once, she forced herself to move forward, caught between a killer who could be lurking out front and a man who had inexplicably developed the ability to turn her thoughts inside out.

If she was going to survive this, she needed the old Wyatt to reappear, the one who consistently jumped on her last nerve and gave her the side-eye like he expected her to steal his great-grandmother's prized silver soup ladle. This Wyatt made no sense. A nice guy who was willing to put himself between her and a bullet if needed was almost as frightening as the man who'd charged into her life and tried to kidnap her the night before, albeit in a completely different way.

Jenna planted her hands on her hips. "I took care of myself for years before you decided to ride in and play hero. I'll be fine now. Just keep out of my way today." She headed for the front room, her words stinging her own ears as his hand fell away.

He said nothing.

Sure, she'd been harsh, but this tone was exactly how she'd spoken to Wyatt for years. No holds barred, no filter, no sugar coating. The moment of "normal" should have made her feel better. Instead, it left her feeling like a complete shrew.

He followed her into the main room, keeping his distance a few paces. "I guess you took the whole act-like-nothing's-different speech to heart." His voice was flat.

She should apologize, should confess the way this new normal was messing with her head as much as the fact her anonymity had been shattered and she had no idea who'd done it. Trying to figure out what to say, she rounded the corner of the bar and stopped, her mouth nearly dropping open.

The mess she'd dreaded cleaning was gone. No dried blue paint marred the pristine metal counter. No random bottles were scattered around the space.

She turned and scanned the far wall, near the door. The paint racks were organized, each bottle filled, each resting in its proper place. Clean brushes stood in jars, fresh trays were stacked high beneath the paints and pristine canvases leaned in their racks against the wall. There was nothing to do but flip the open sign and unlock the door.

Jenna closed her mouth, then looked to Wyatt. "Who did this?"

"Our guys cleared out early this morning. Erin texted me around three and said she had a group of ladies from the church who wanted to know if there was anything they could do to help. I guess they heard about what happened when I called in the men to fix your door." He pinned her gaze with his, his voice intimate, almost like a caress, even from across the room. "I told you earlier, you have a lot of people in this town who care about you."

"Does that include you?"

His head jerked, and he glanced at the front window, then to her, his expression tight and professional. "My job is to keep you safe." Breaking the gaze, he turned and walked to the front window, where he stood ramrod straight, surveying the empty street.

Her cheeks heated. Why in the world had she asked such a loaded question? Of course he was doing his job. This was Wyatt the Noble. He wasn't going to let personal feelings interfere with his work, even if his work was keeping her out of harm's way. The kind of cool tolerance that had marked their relationship from the beginning didn't disappear overnight.

Forget it. With her mind heavy under the weight of her precarious position, she needed to let Wyatt be Wyatt. Besides, she'd gotten exactly what she wished for a few minutes earlier—the status quo, the rebalancing of their relationship to what it had been twenty-four hours before.

So why didn't it feel as comforting as she'd assumed it would?

It was too much to think about. Jenna glanced at the time on her phone, fired off a quick thank-you text to Erin, then flicked the mouse on the computer. She needed to stay busy, to keep moving. Until the customers started coming in about an hour and a half from now, there was little to do other than finalize the previous day's receipts, a job she hadn't been able to get to the night before.

The email indicator flashed at the bottom of the screen, and she clicked to make sure there was nothing pressing. The first message in the list blared its subject line in all caps. READ ME FIRST, AMY.

Jenna gasped and backed away from the computer, knocking the wireless mouse to the floor.

Wyatt was at her side before she could catch her breath, his hand between her shoulder blades. "What happened?"

There wasn't enough air to make words. Jenna couldn't tear her eyes away from her sister's name. Her *dead* sister's name.

Tension radiated off Wyatt as he leaned closer to the screen. "Amy? Your sister?"

"Yes."

He bent forward and retrieved the mouse, then turned to Jenna. "Do I have your permission to open it?"

She nodded as the shaking started in her chest and moved out to her fingers. Jenna wrapped her arms around her middle. She was so cold. Why would someone think Amy was alive?

Maybe it was an advertisement.

But, no. If this was spam, it was the worst, most ill-timed spam ever.

Wyatt slipped his arm around her waist and held her against his side, his warmth transferring to her, supporting her. He clicked on the email.

Thought you could hide? Not from us. There's a cell phone attached to the back of the dumpster in the alley. Be at the location on the GPS by 10:30 this morning. Leave your cell phone on the counter. No police. If you don't follow instructions, the offer to turn yourself over alive expires.

Wyatt's hand slipped to the small of her back and edged her around the counter, away from the computer. "In your office. Now." He dragged her with him, easing her in front of him so he stood between the front windows and her as they hurried across the main room to her office.

Jenna stumbled and barely caught the door frame before Wyatt crowded her into the office and around the desk. "Sit." He stayed in the doorway, watching the two-way mirror that looked out into the main room. His mouth was a hard line, his eyes serious and professional—it was a glimpse of the police officer he was and the soldier he'd once been. His hand hovered near his hip as though he expected to draw quickly, but then he pulled out his phone and tapped out a message. He mumbled, "It's close to eight thirty now. Two hours."

"I don't understand." Jenna's voice trembled. "Why does someone think my sister's alive? Why would someone think I'm her?"

"There's a different question you need to ask." He scrubbed a hand along his jaw and turned from the window, his expression grim. "Why would someone want your sister dead?"

SIX

Jenna gasped, but Wyatt turned away. She needed a second to process, but he couldn't give her the space, not while maintaining his position between her and danger. The best he could do was to look away and give her a bit of privacy.

He stood in the doorway to Jenna's office and swiveled his head from side to side. Back door. Front windows.

Back door. The monitor over the door revealed an empty alley, the space immediately by the door in view but nothing else. Without a wider shot, there was no way to know if anyone lurked beyond the steps.

Front windows. Very few people on the street. Nobody passing turned to look into Jenna's darkened store front.

But somewhere, somebody was watching.

His phone vibrated and he glanced at the screen. Forward email and all headers to me. Feds want to see. Sit tight. Getting men into position near you. Find out all you can from Jenna.

Lowering his phone, Wyatt turned to find Jenna staring at him. He'd seen the stubborn look she now wore many times when she was determined to go toe-to-toe with him over something. The last time had been right in this room, when he'd had to inform Erin that a killer had been in her house.

In spite of the situation, he nearly smiled. Jenna had accused him of lacking tact. He'd ignored her mostly because he didn't want to admit she was right.

Now Jenna's look of bold determination was working for him, not against him. She stood and drew back her shoulders, probably trying to make herself feel taller. Young soldiers often did the same.

"What do we do?" Her voice trembled, betraying her fear. "Don't tell me you don't know. You're on your phone. You're making plans. I said I'd help, so if you're going to force me to go on the run, I want to know." The last words shook worse than the first.

She didn't want to leave. She really did love this town, these people.

It took everything he had not to close the space to her desk and sweep her against him, to make her promises he could never keep about protecting her, about making sure her home remained her home.

Instead, he ran his thumb along the screen of his phone by his thigh and kept his eyes on hers. "Hang tight. We're not alone. There are officers getting into place right now. They're not going to leave us hanging. Somebody will give us a next move soon." He had a sinking feeling he knew exactly what the next move was going to be, and he wasn't sure how he'd fight if "the powers that be" wanted to use Jenna as bait.

He couldn't reveal any of his thoughts or fears to her now, though. The chief had given him an assignment.

Get answers from the notoriously tight-lipped woman in front of him. Finding out all he could about her sister was job one.

Well, job two. Job one was making sure Jenna survived.

Purposely relaxing his shoulders, Wyatt pulled out the chair across the desk from her and settled in, trying to project a calm he didn't feel. He didn't say anything, just hoped she'd follow his lead.

For a moment, it looked as though she was going to stay on her feet glaring at him. A number of emotions crossed her face before she sank into her chair and dragged it to the desk, still eyeballing him. "You're over there planning something. You can't possibly be this calm."

Wyatt threw his plans out the window. He should have known better than to try to fool Jenna. She saw through him every time, and it was clear subtle questions weren't going to work. He would have to come at her head-on. "I need to know everything about your sister."

The statement didn't seem to surprise her, although she stiffened. "Amy's dead. Nothing I say is going to change anything. All of the facts in the world won't give you clues about why someone thinks I'm her."

"You were twins. It's an easy mistake."

"Except...she's...dead." The assertion came through gritted teeth.

"I understand." He slid to the edge of the wooden chair and sat forward, resting his hands on his knees. No doubt her sister's death still made her ache. He needed to think this through. *Direct* didn't have to mean *in-delicate.*

Tact. She'd reminded him before he needed it. Neither of them had ever dreamed he'd need it with her. "I know it's not easy to talk about, but there might be a clue you don't see. I've got fresh eyes. Let me help."

The fight left Jenna and she sank against her chair, gripping the arms. She rocked the chair silently from side to side. "I'll do my best."

"Let's start with when and how Amy died."

Jenna kept her eyes on the desk in front of her, the lines in her forehead deepening. She ran her finger along the edge of the huge calendar covering the scarred wood on her desk. "I'd been here about six months. No contact with anyone from El Paso, not even Amy... Not that we'd been in contact before I left. Anthony told me when I ran to keep from reaching out because one slip could lead Logan right to me, assuming he was even interested. Amy and I had been estranged for almost a year and..." Her expression tightened, as though she was trying to hold tears at bay. Her voice strained. "I got an envelope in the mail two years ago." She leaned over and reached into her bottom desk drawer, then withdrew a folder that appeared to be filled with receipts and tax papers. She extracted a battered-looking sheet of newspaper and handed it across the desk.

Wyatt unfolded it carefully. It had been handled often. The torn edges were soft. Something wet had dotted the page and been allowed to dry, leaving spots across the headline. One Dead in Hit-and-Run. A large color photo revealed a car nearly torn in half by a telephone pole. Further into the article, a photo was set into the text. The woman was a mirror of Jenna, although her hair was lighter, her face leaner. It appeared to be a head shot from a website and identified the woman as Amy Brady of Porter Street in El Paso.

Brady. He lifted his head and studied Jenna, whose eyes were on the clipping he held. "Was Amy married?"

"Briefly. He was killed in combat."

Not the man who was coming after her then. He texted the new information to the chief and rested his phone on his leg. "Was there anything else with the article?"

Jenna's hand went to her throat, then her fingers trailed to tug at the chain around her neck, hesitantly revealing a small charm. From where he sat, Wyatt couldn't quite make it out, but it was silver, some sort of flower.

"The necklace was in the envelope? What is it?"

"It was Amy's. She always wore it." There was a sheen of tears in Jenna's eyes. "I gave it to her for Christmas one year."

So someone had had access to Amy's body? Why? *Tact, Wyatt.* He couldn't ask such a callous question. It would surely wreck her. They could discuss the necklace another time. "Who sent it?"

"I don't know. Maybe Anthony? No one else knew where to find me. The postmark's from Indiana, but he probably sent it to a friend, who sent it to another friend and so on."

"And you're certain Anthony wouldn't be involved in this?"

"He was the only man who ever cared about me and Amy. He did what he could for us while he could. He snuck into the hospital to help me when he heard what Logan did to me. It can't be Anthony. Look somewhere else."

"I need his last name. We need to be certain—"

"No." The denial was firm, hard.

Wyatt's neck burned with the impatient anger he was fighting to keep in check. If he kept pushing, she'd stop talking. For now, he had to let this one slide, but he'd definitely be passing along the first name. The Feds could dig deeper than anyone in the Mountain Springs department.

"Okay, fine. I need to know anything that would point me to why someone thinks Amy's alive. Where did she work? Who were her friends?"

"How is this helping?" Jenna stood and walked to the window.

The urge to jerk her away from the glass was almost enough to bring Wyatt to his feet. Instead, he prayed the two-way mirror kept her screened from anyone outside.

She paced to her chair, allowing Wyatt to breathe again. "Somebody expects me to walk out the back door, grab a cell phone off a dumpster and meet them in less than two hours. Can't we trap them? As soon as I grab the phone, you'll know exactly where they're going to be and you can just—just…go get them." She aimed a finger at the door. "We're wasting time."

"No. You're giving me information to pass on and help the men and women outside put together a plan to catch them. I understand you're frustrated. So am I."

She had no idea. If he was in charge, he'd have already packed her things and moved her to a safe house. Let the Feds sort out who was behind this. At least Jenna would be out of the crosshairs.

"Fine." With a hefty sigh, Jenna leaned against the wall behind her chair and crossed her arms, probably too restless to sit. "She worked at a place called New Horizons Day Spa. She was a personal trainer and an assistant manager. Up until Logan managed to steer me away from her, I'm not sure she had friends outside of work. In fact, she's the one who introduced me…" Jenna's jaw slackened, her eyes growing wide. "She was friends with Logan."

Jenna grabbed the back of her chair and stared at Wyatt, unseeing.

"Jenna." Wyatt's voice was low. He set his phone on the desk and leaned closer. "Talk to me."

"Yesterday I was probably the safest I've ever been. I had friends, a job I love, a place to live that feels like a home… Now I've never been in more danger. And my sister? She might be connected to—"

His phone buzzed and she stopped, watching, her lips tight. She knew as well as he did what was coming.

And neither of them was ready.

Team's in place. Have Jenna go get the phone.

The timing was terrible. He tapped his thumb on the screen. Do we have a minute?

There wasn't a pause. No.

One word. No choice.

Jenna pushed away from her chair on shaky legs,

her earlier determined demeanor set into place. She was very, very good at slipping behind her carefully crafted mask. "I can do this. If it will put a stop to everything, I can do it."

Earlier, when she'd first seen the email with her sister's name in the subject line, the instinct to put his arm around her and be her strength had propelled him with a force he couldn't resist. He'd never felt the drive to protect so strongly.

This moment dwarfed everything else. Jenna shouldn't be a target in a game where no one even knew who their opponent was. The urge to pack her into his truck and drive as far out of town as he could built in his chest until it almost cut off his air.

"Jen, you don't have to go. Say the word and we can wave off, get you somewhere safe, somewhere away from here. The team can snag the phone, move in on the chance the bad guys are already at the location. We can hide you until—"

"Seriously?" She jerked her head, a strand of hair catching one of her eyelashes. "What happened to 'you don't have to run, Jenna' and 'we all have your back, Jenna'?"

"I said those things before, when I thought we were dealing with a crazy ex-boyfriend. There are too many unknowns. Let me take you somewhere safe." Wyatt stood, desperate to make her see logic. The thought of her walking into some psycho's crosshairs ate at his gut in a way he'd never imagined it would. She had no idea what was coming next, but he did. They'd have her get the phone, then they'd have her go to the rendezvous point alone. She'd be trailed by the Feds but she'd still be alone. Anything could happen, even with a federal team feet away.

Jenna shook her head and stood and smoothed the front of her jeans, then eased around him to look out the two-way mirror into the front of the store. "I want this finished. I don't want to leave Mountain Springs. If there's even a remote chance I can keep my life here—"

"Listen to reason." Wyatt blocked her path to the door. "If you—" His phone vibrated.

She turned. "What do they say?"

Lord, let it be we've somehow already caught them, and this is all finished before it even starts. Wyatt lifted the phone and read the screen out loud. "'Move out. Now.'"

With time short, there wasn't room to bring in reinforcements or decoys. Jenna would have to walk out the back door of the building, retrieve the device and drive to the rendezvous point.

Alone.

The whole thing was risky, dangerous, but there hadn't been time to plan anything else. The FBI wanted these guys as badly as Wyatt did.

Lifting her chin, Jenna moved to edge around Wyatt and out the door. She pulled her car keys from her pocket and gripped them tightly.

As she passed, he slid sideways and blocked her, their faces mere inches apart. He scanned her green eyes and the small scar at her hairline, then let his gaze brush hers. His heart hammered harder. At some point last night, while he'd held her until the shaking stopped, his life had shifted. Jenna was a friend. Her protective instinct for her sister resonated with him, linking them.

She didn't deserve to be hurt.

Her eyes widened, then became hooded before she laid a hand on his arm and brushed past, headed for the door. "Just pray, Wyatt."

She stopped at the door, her hand on the knob, and straightened her shoulders, once again slipping into the false front she wore too well. Without turning back, Jenna went to the back door, opened it and stepped into the alley out of his line of sight.

A sharp crack and a metallic ping crashed into the building.

Jenna cried out in pain as the door slipped shut.

Wyatt ran, glancing into the corner at the security monitor, but the angle gave a view of the steps alone.

He jerked open the door, aware too late the next shot could have his name on it, and bolted down the steps, nearly tripping over Jenna, who was lying in a motionless heap on the pavement.

SEVEN

Frantic shouts. Footsteps. Distant radio transmissions.

Jenna curled into a tighter ball and huddled next to her car. Someone had shot at her. She'd walked out the door and someone…had…

A hand pressed into her back, and the familiar clean scent of Wyatt's soap filtered through the haze as he leaned close. "You okay? Were you hit?"

Wyatt was here. She was safe. Trying to calm her rapid breathing, Jenna inventoried her limbs. The only pain was in her knees, where she'd dropped to the ground like a ball of wet clay. "No. I'm okay." She dared to lift her head and look at Wyatt.

He was crouched beside her, one knee on the ground, his pistol drawn and held at the ready in his right hand. His left hand still rested on her back. His dark blue eyes scanned the alley, from side to side, from top to bottom.

The radio on his shoulder crackled. "Suspect apprehended."

There were more words, but the buzzing in her ears wouldn't let her hear them. Jenna rocked onto her heels then turned, drew her knees to her chest and sagged against her car. "They got him?"

Still on one knee in front of Jenna, Wyatt holstered his pistol, nodded once, then let his eyes sweep her face, her arms, her legs as though he didn't quite believe she was telling the truth when she said she was uninjured. He rested a finger on her knee, sending a stinging, shooting pain along her leg and into her hip. "You tore your jeans."

Jenna leaned forward to inspect the damage, her hair brushing his cheek. "If a hole in my jeans is the worst thing to happen to me today—"

"Come on. I want to get you inside. Just in case." Staying low and keeping himself between Jenna and the alley, Wyatt ushered her inside and shut the heavy metal door behind them, twisting the lock before he guided her into her office.

She was settled in her chair, safe from spying eyes and flying bullets, when the shaking started. Her stomach rolled and quaked, seeming to reverberate throughout her body until her hands and knees shook with the tremors.

Wyatt opened the mini fridge wedged between a bookcase and the wall, found a bottle of water then brought it to her, cracking it open before he reached for her hand and wrapped her fingers around the bottle. "Drink. Your nerves will settle in a minute."

Her teeth knocked together. "Need coffee. Warmth. Not cold. Shivering."

"I get it." He graced her with a reassuring smile then knelt in front of her, pressing her hand so she lifted the bottle. "Drink something. I promise we'll get you some coffee in a little bit. Decaf."

His teasing brought a slight smile. Jenna managed to drink a couple of sips without letting water dribble down her chin. Thankfully. Even with everything happening outside, drooling in front of Wyatt felt like it would be a catastrophe of epic proportions.

His phone buzzed, too loud against her frayed nerves.

Jenna jumped and squeezed the water bottle, cold water shooting onto her jeans and Wyatt's shirt. Her teeth dug into her lip, her cheeks heating. "I'm—"

He shook his head with a slight smile, then grew serious as he read the text, then stood. "I'm going to let the chief in. It won't take but a second." His gaze lingered on hers as though he was considering something before he turned and walked out of the office.

Jenna watched him go, then set the water bottle on her desk and dropped her head into her hands. She ought to be scared. Terrified. Already running. Other than the tremors from the shock, she felt nothing. Numb. Empty. It was as though her emotions had overloaded and blown a fuse.

She'd felt such a deep, hollow darkness one other time, when Logan's first blow landed against her cheek. The sheer shock of it had somehow managed to knock her mind loose from her body. If she wasn't taking it all the way in, maybe it wasn't really happening.

Wyatt walked into the room with the chief and two other people behind him. Her heart stuttered, then fired a rapid rhythm even she couldn't decipher. If this didn't end soon, nobody would have to kill her. She'd land her own self in the hospital.

Four people in her minuscule office packed the room and stifled the oxygen. Wyatt edged around the desk to stand beside her, while Chief Thompson and the man and woman who'd followed him in took positions near the door. The woman wore faded jeans and a T-shirt featuring a band from the bluegrass festival. She didn't look a day over twenty. The man looked like an ad for hipsters, from his beard to his hiking boots. She didn't recognize either of them from around town. Probably the federal team. FBI? Homeland Security? Both? Everything Wyatt had told her leaked from her mind and left her empty.

Arch Thompson studied Jenna for a long moment before he sat in the chair in front of her, propping his ankle on his knee and settling in like he was on his mama's front porch ready for a long chat. All he lacked was a tall glass of sweet tea.

Chief Thompson was like that. Every time Jenna had met him, he'd been friendly, laid-back, helpful. Though he was barely four years older than she was, he approached his job with a serious work ethic and quiet humor as well. With his dark hair, even darker eyes and athletic build, it was no wonder half of the single women in Mountain Springs had set their sights on him.

Today, more than ever, Jenna appreciated the way nothing ever seemed to rile him up or surprise him. His presence and demeanor settled a calm over the room, a sharp contrast to the two strangers who stood by the door and studied her as though she was hiding something.

Sort of the same way Wyatt used to look at her.

As though he knew she'd thought of him, Wyatt rested a hand on her shoulder. "The chief has a few questions."

Nobody moved to introduce the strangers. Jenna didn't ask. Instead, she focused on Chief Thompson. "I have no idea who's doing this or why they're doing it."

"I don't doubt it. None of us do." He glanced over his shoulder at the agents in the doorway then turned to Jenna. "Can they get a look at your computer?"

She nodded once. "It's out front." She scribbled the password on a sticky note and passed it across the desk to the chief, who handed it over his shoulder to the woman. "This password logs you in to the main system. My email is already open."

"We need your phone as well." The female agent took the device, then looked at Jenna again. "Social media?"

"I don't have any." Too risky. One loose picture of her out on the internet could have led Logan right to her.

If he had even been looking. She wasn't sure of anything anymore.

Jenna pressed her fingers to her temples and kneaded the tension building there. "Somebody thinks I'm my sister."

"Officer Stephens told me in his texts. You want to fill me in on the story?" Arch pulled a notebook from his belt and poised a pen to write.

Still numb, Jenna recited the bare facts to him, the

same ones she'd told Wyatt less than half an hour earlier, ending with "I don't understand."

The chief tapped his pen against the arm of the chair, his dark gaze set on Jenna. "Tell me about the man who ran the gym where your sister worked."

She blinked. What? This was about her sister, not about...

Her stomach twisted as realization dipped the roller coaster into a whole new loop. Another twist. Another segment of her life was no longer what it had always appeared to be. She looked up over her shoulder at Wyatt. "Logan was... You said he was making deliveries all over Texas." At his nod, she turned to the chief. "He delivered and maintained equipment for New Horizons Day Spa and they had locations all over Texas. Logan Cutter was working with New Horizons. What do you know about the owner?"

Chief Thompson said nothing, simply kept a level gaze on Jenna, waiting.

"I think..." Jenna had met the spa's owner once, when she worked part-time one summer at the mall, getting people to register for week-long free trials. He'd come by the kiosk, chatted briefly, given her a hearty handshake, then disappeared. At the time, he'd appeared to be nothing more than a charming, friendly, regular guy. A normal business owner working a normal job.

She swiped her hand on her jeans, still feeling his touch. Now that she knew what he'd been doing behind the scenes, his touch burned through distance and time. "His name was Grant...Meyer?" She shook her head.

"I saw him one time, and it was briefly. He had a lot of locations around Texas so he was rarely in El Paso."

The chief closed his notebook, shoved it into the pocket on his belt and leaned closer to the desk. "Jenna, we need to talk about something."

Her chin rose, defenses rising at the gravity in his tone. Whatever he was about to say, it wasn't good.

"The FBI and DHS suspected Logan Cutter and Grant Meyer of trafficking for quite some time, but they never had proof, not until someone at the El Paso location approached a local team with information. This witness had found a paper trail, evidence the federal government needed to build a case."

The ensuing silence spoke loudly. Pride and grief rose in Jenna's chest, nearly cutting off her words. "My sister turned them in."

Wyatt's fingers tightened on her shoulder as Arch nodded. "They've long believed her death was no accident, had a belief somehow either Cutter or Meyer figured out who the leak was and they retaliated."

Jenna stiffened and turned her head away from the chief. Her sister. Murdered by a man she'd trusted. A man who had been murdered as well. "I don't…" Her tongue was heavy and thick. Everything seemed to run together in a sick shade of lifeless gray. "My life is not a movie."

"We know." Wyatt's voice cut through the goop in her brain, but barely.

It felt like a movie. A convoluted, twisted thriller with a plot spinning out of control. Her brain had detached, deciding to watch everything from the outside.

How had she landed in a place where revenge killings, snipers and mistaken identity marked her? To the FBI and Homeland Security standing inside her shop, scrolling through her computer?

Chief Thompson sat back and crossed his arms over his chest. "We need you to consider some sort of protection detail, some place to hide. FBI and DHS aren't ready to move you into a safe house, but after what's happened here this morning, I'd like to get you out of sight."

Jenna shoved back her chair and turned on Wyatt, a pent-up tornado of emotions unleashed. "You said you'd protect me, and you'd keep me safe. You said I wouldn't have to leave."

He held both hands out between them. "You don't have to do anything you don't want to do."

Chief Thompson stood as well. He towered over her, although he likely didn't mean to look as intimidating as he did. Without turning away from her, he addressed Wyatt. "Stephens, give us a minute."

He stiffened, clearly wanting to argue, but with a curt "Yes, sir," he stepped out of the room. The back door slammed a few seconds later.

There was no questioning why the chief had sent Wyatt out. Jenna stared at her shoes. "You know."

"The Feds briefed me. They've known for a while who you really are. It didn't take much to connect you to your *twin* sister."

"Does Wyatt know?"

"I'm the only person in town who does, and I'll keep

it that way for as long as you want. The Feds are willing to as well."

"Why?" She should feel relieved, but she didn't. What she and Anthony had done to forge her new identity had to be illegal. How could they ignore it?

"I have no idea, and I'm not asking. It's worked to keep you safe this far, so I suppose they intend to go with the status quo. I'll be ordering Wyatt and the others to stop any investigation and to focus on protection alone. He'll be in charge of moving you out of town."

"But—"

"No arguments. We've had three incidents happen in downtown now, Jenna. Last night here and at your apartment, now today… I'm not comfortable with snipers firing off rounds in the middle of the busiest week of the year, when we're packed with locals and tourists."

Jenna sank into her chair, defeat dragging her low. He was right. As long as she was in the open, she was a danger to everyone in the town she loved. What she wanted no longer mattered.

Once again, the life she knew was obliterated.

"If you need anything, let me know." Christa Naylor hovered in the doorway of her small studio, watching Jenna with a practiced eye. Dust danced in the harsh overhead fluorescent lights, which cast shadows on Christa's weather-worn face yet somehow made her long gray braid glow with a silvery light. "Are you sure you're okay?"

It was easy to tell the older woman had been a criminal psychologist before she retired to Mountain Springs, bringing her pottery wheel and a full store of empathy with her. She'd seen more than enough of the evil in the world while working with the State Bureau of Investigations, and she'd likely never dreamed she'd be called into action again, even briefly. While Jenna had never told Christa the truth about her past, she'd unburdened herself to her friend on more than one occasion, always sticking to feelings over facts. Jenna had sought refuge at Christa's many times, borrowing quiet time at the pottery wheel in an attempt to recapture the essence of the real Genevieve Brady, who still lived inside her.

Now, this refuge might save her life.

Christa had planted her pottery wheel inside an old fallout shelter sliced into the mountain behind her house. The rough stone walls of the small room offered a hiding place few people knew existed, but one that Chief Thompson viewed as a natural place for Jenna to seek shelter.

If only he knew this shelter might also save her sanity. Familiar, warm… Maybe God was still looking out for her after all, placing her in the one place on earth that could protect her and even bring a sliver of peace to her weary soul.

"Jenna? I asked if you're okay."

"I'm fine." Well, there was a whopper if she'd ever told one. Her hands still shook from the strike of the bullet against the antique brick in the alley. Her mind still whirled through the horrors of traffickers, betrayal, murder…

"It's not every day someone gets put in the crosshairs, you know."

"I know." Jenna ran a finger along the lump of clay she'd placed in the center of the pottery wheel. Guilt gnawed at her stomach. Look what she'd brought to a tiny town that was still adjusting to a growing tourist trade. She'd brought more than petty crime. She'd brought men who cared nothing about collateral damage on their hunt for a woman who was, tragically, already dead.

"I'm fine," Jenna repeated. "Being here might do more for me than anything in the world."

"Anytime." Resting a weathered hand against the door frame, Christa glanced over her shoulder. "You're in good hands with Officer Stephens outside watching out, so I'll head inside. This can't be easy for you. I've talked to too many victims who thought they were okay when they weren't. If you want to talk, my door's always open." With a two-fingered wave, Christa ducked out, pulling the door shut and sealing out the natural light.

Victims. The connotations of that word were too frightening to dwell on. Instead, Jenna exhaled and glanced around the stark room. It wasn't the most creative space, but it was quiet and cool. There was only one way in, through the door Wyatt currently guarded.

She'd asked him to stay outside, to give her time to process. Even one of the events of the past twenty-four hours would have sent her into a freak-out. Added all together? She was scared to breathe for fear something would change before she could exhale.

Jenna adjusted the stool and inched closer to the wheel, eyeing the wedged clay she'd lumped into the center. There was no vision in her head, no idea of how to form the shapeless mass. All she knew was it would be a gift to have her fingers coated in water and clay, to pretend the world outside this hollowed-out crevice in the side of Casey Mountain didn't exist.

She flipped the switch to set the wheel spinning slowly at first, dampened her fingers and let them run along the clay, shaping nothing, simply getting the feel of the material, letting her fingers sink in where they wanted, easing the pressure when it felt right. Jenna lost herself in the glory of creation, of the moment she got to feel a fraction of what God must have felt when He shaped Adam. Jenna was lost in prayers focused on her Lord and thoughts focused on her work.

A tap at the door sunk her thumb in too deeply and she jerked, then flipped the switch beneath the wheel.

The door slipped open, revealing afternoon sunlight and Wyatt. "Is it okay to come in?"

Her heart drove harder at the shock of seeing him. He wasn't supposed to come in until dinnertime. She glanced at her watch and her eyes widened. She'd been deep into her work for almost an hour.

All she had to show was a formless something, a deep gouge working a ring around the center. It didn't really matter. The clay was an overworked mess, wet and soggy.

Wyatt shut the door behind him, eyeing her work. "Well, I'm no art critic, but what you've got there is definitely…different."

"Yeah. Sometimes it's more about the feeling than the art." Jenna pressed her palms against the small of her back, suddenly aware she'd been hunched for too long. Her shoulders ached, a reminder that she didn't do this every day anymore. Muscle memory might be a real thing, but so was fatigue.

Wyatt hefted a white paper bag. "I wasn't sure if you'd be hungry, so I called Erin to see what you liked. Officer Early was off this morning, but he brought this out with him when he returned from checking on Nina."

"Is she okay?" Jenna didn't know Brian Early well, but his sister often came in to the shop to paint.

"She was sick so he went to check on her."

Jenna started to say more, but her stomach stopped her. She hadn't considered food before and really didn't want to now. The spicy scent of a burrito from Enrique's would normally have her reaching for the bag, but it wasn't working today. "Not hungry right now, but it was nice of you to bring me something, Stephens." Her words held light bravado, but the truth was his actions humbled her. Clearly, she'd read him wrong from the beginning. He wasn't a self-centered, arrogant, by-the-book cop.

He was the opposite... Well, except for the by-the-book thing. He'd been nothing but kind, selfless and giving ever since he'd rescued her. Jenna wanted to apologize for every sharp word said in the past, but he turned and set the bag on a table in the corner, severing the moment. "I can leave it here until you're ready. I'll be outside if you—"

"Can you stay?"

Wyatt turned slowly, looking as if he needed her to repeat the question.

Yeah, she'd surprised herself, too. "If you need to be

outside where you can keep an eye out, I understand, but…" She waved a hand coated in rapidly drying clay. "I've been by myself for a while. I could use a friendly face." Wow. She'd never imagined she'd consider Wyatt's face a friendly one, but here they were.

Well, here he was.

He hesitated before he grabbed a metal chair. Settling it across the wheel from her, he straddled it and crossed his arms on the low back. He didn't look at her but kept his eyes on the clay she'd been working. "Is this the first time you've done this?"

The first time? Jenna laughed. The release felt good. Honestly, she had no idea why the question was funny, but it tickled something inside her and gave her a moment in the purest sense of who she was. This afternoon had been good for her, had run a sense of self through her hands along her arms and into her soul. "No."

"This is funny because…?" The question at the end of Wyatt's sentence lifted right along with his right eyebrow.

It was adorable.

Jenna swallowed, then wet her hands and smashed the clay into a shapeless lump again. Maybe she'd leave it the way it was and fire it as a giant blob. It was already overworked and useless, but it sure was representative of her emotions. Someday, it could be a good reminder of…

Never mind. She didn't want or need a reminder of any of this. Except maybe of Wyatt's new friendship.

Her brain felt unsatisfied. If she walked away from the wheel without some release of her creativity, she'd be restless and anxious for the rest of the night. Jenna scraped the clay from the wheel and centered a fresh mound of clay, then turned the wheel on slowly at first, letting the noise and the rotation draw her in. She let her fingers work, easing the speed on the wheel as the image in her mind took shape. Still, it never really overtook her awareness of Wyatt's question in the air, or his eyes on her hands.

Even with his scrutiny, Jenna felt not one iota of self-consciousness. Wyatt watching her work seemed to be the most natural thing in the world, like something they'd shared a million times.

He let his earlier question slide, and Jenna couldn't calculate how long they sat in silence, her shaping, him watching, before he spoke again. "You're making a coffee mug."

"Yes." Their first real, personal and friendly conversation was on her mind, the night he'd admired her work without knowing it was hers. Genuine admiration, not fake because he had no idea she'd made it. The candor made his comments precious. "I am."

He leaned closer, avoiding the splashes of clay and mud thrown out by the wheel, and studied the piece as it spun between them. "It's familiar."

Easing the pressure so her fingers lightly rested on the clay, Jenna forced her breathing into rhythm. There was something about him watching, about breathing the same air. His presence crept under her skin and thrummed in her heart.

Wyatt cleared his throat and eased away, keeping his eyes on her hands.

The air was instantly easier to breathe. It was also much colder.

"Those mugs at your apartment... You made those?"

"Mmm-hmm." Jenna didn't trust her voice or her hands. She was overwrought and emotional. There was no other reason for her heart to stutter. She shifted and tilted her neck to one side, then returned to her work, narrowing the neck of the mug slightly before fanning out the lip.

"Why not tell me?"

"Because the person who made those mugs is who I used to be. Who I've had to hide all this time. I've not been able to let anyone know Jenna Clark is really an artist." It felt good to tell the truth, to remember out loud some of the real self she'd left behind.

"You're an artist? Like the folks around town? You made pottery and people bought it, even recommended their friends buy it?"

"Sounds funny to say it the way you did, but yes. I had a studio in El Paso, but I did business all over the state. Custom designs and such." She frowned and watched the lip of the mug roll under her fingertips. Once she escaped, Logan's generosity in building her a studio in his sunroom made too much sense. It had kept her close, inside, tied to him.

"Hmm." Wyatt gripped the chair's back and stretched his arms, his eyes finally finding hers. "So if I couldn't sleep one night and I got bored and I did an internet search for you—"

"If you searched for Jenna Clark, you won't find a thing."

Her heart drummed, pounding a rhythm from her chest into her fingertips. The electricity in this conversation was about to make her hair stand on end. She was dancing in a place she hadn't danced in years, around the thing she'd buried and assumed she'd never speak of again.

The truth.

"You specialized in word of mouth?" Wyatt's eyes sparked with amusement. He was enjoying this, though Jenna had no idea why. It wasn't like he really cared. "I get it. You were one of those mysterious artists who used a riddle to build their brand. You don't find Jenna Clark. Jenna Clark finds you."

Mouth dry, Jenna scratched her cheek on her shoulder. She kept her focus on her hands and the delicate finishing work she was doing, but her fingers shook so much she stopped and reached down to flip the power switch. If she kept going, she'd ruin the piece that spoke her heart, a coffee mug that had sparked in her imagination, one that would burn from fiery red at the bottom to cool in ocean blue at the lip.

Was she really going to do this?

One glance at Wyatt, one shot of his expression, which was slowly shifting from amused to concerned, and she knew. Yes, she was. She owed him. After all he'd done for her, she owed him the truest part of herself.

"You won't find anything under Jenna Clark."

"Okay…"

"Jenna Clark is not my real name." She sniffed, turned her gaze to the ceiling and traced the cobwebs there. It was too late to turn back now.

And she wasn't sure she wanted to.

EIGHT

Wyatt watched Jenna as she scanned the ceiling. She was either sorry she'd said too much or was searching for answers in the rock above her head.

Either way, his mouth wrestled with his mind. She was about to tell him something with the potential to blow her case wide open and he wanted to urge her on, stop her silence before she changed her mind and retreated. His entire being strained toward her, but he forced himself to be still and wait for her to come around to the words for herself. If he pushed, she'd retreat behind the wall she'd built around her life, the one he had managed to crack at some point in the past twenty-four hours.

When the wall had cracked, it had also shattered nearly every preconception he'd held about Jenna. Yes, she was hiding something and his subconscious had rankled about it since the day he met her. But she wasn't malicious. She was brave, tenacious and determined to survive.

There had been so much for her to have to survive, and she spoke of her life as though her past was normal.

She was stronger than anyone he'd ever met.

As his admiration for her grew, however, he couldn't forget she was an assignment. His job was not only to keep her safe from whoever believed she was her sister, but also to find out everything she knew so the federal agents could continue with their investigation.

Guilt ran a thread through his conscience. He wasn't being completely honest with her, but he couldn't be, not if he wanted the truth. Not if he was keeping the bigger picture in mind, bringing traffickers to justice and stopping them from infiltrating his beloved hometown.

Jenna slowly turned the pottery wheel, inspecting each side of the mug she'd formed so deftly, seemingly without thought. "I don't mark my pottery. Not anymore."

"Because somebody could use it to find you."

"I had to take a break from art in general for a while. The only person in town who knows I throw pottery is Christa." She sliced a glance at him. "Long story how she found out about it all."

"I'm listening." His voice strained. *Come on, Jenna. What's the whole story? What is it you really want to say?* He had to keep her talking. "So you thought a paint-your-own-canvas shop was enough distance from the real you? Pretty risky, if you're trying to hide your passion for art."

"Not so much." She ghosted a smile as she smoothed an edge gently with her thumb, her focus on the mug. "I used to be a bit of a snob." Her thumb hesitated and she lifted a slight smile before she resumed her work. "I told Logan frequently how I thought paint-your-own-pottery, or canvas, or whatever stores counted as pseudo art and wasn't truly art at all. It was fake, not for real, gifted artists." She'd finished the sentence with a semi-British accent then sniffed, her smile bitter. "Now that I've been running the shop for a while, I know… Everybody has an artistic fire inside of them, not just me. God created all of us, and creation is a joy to Him. I think He's given everyone an innate desire to create beauty, but all of us have different talents for doing it. Painting is a fun way to bring it out, especially for our generation, who got to watch Bob Ross paint mountains and birds on PBS."

Wyatt chuckled. "True." Only Jenna would drop a pop-culture reference like the painter of "happy little trees" into a conversation like this.

"Letting others be creative while I stand aside has let me see art isn't exclusive. It was horrible of me to think I had the lock on creativity and beauty, that I was somehow the gatekeeper of good taste. So the snob I used to be? Genevieve Brady? She kind of died along with the name."

He couldn't imagine Jenna thinking anything as arrogant as what she described. She seemed so…

Genevieve Brady.

She'd slipped it in under the radar, so he'd nearly missed it. The air in the room stilled, almost as though Jenna waited for him to react.

The truth was, he had no idea how to even think, let alone act. She'd trusted him with the key to who she was, the core of her identity… What was a man supposed to do with a treasure like the one she'd handed him?

He was supposed to turn everything he learned about

her over to Chief Thompson immediately. "Do the Feds know your name?"

"Yes."

Good, then he didn't have to treat this like a clue. Instead, he could sit with this knowledge for a few minutes and treat it with the reverence it deserved.

Genevieve Brady. He let the name roll in his mind. Weighed it, played with it, wondered at it. Since the federal agents already knew, this wasn't a piece of the mystery. This wasn't a new clue to who was after her, or why her pursuers thought her sister was alive.

This was a piece of herself. Freely given. To him.

Part of him wanted to run out the door and hide under one of Christa's prize rosebushes. It was almost too much. Instead, Wyatt cleared his throat. "Genevieve Brady? That's your name?"

Jenna nodded, then lifted the thin disk her handleless coffee mug rested on and walked over to the far wall. A deep cabinet with a lattice door sat there, each shelf housing various drying pottery pieces at evenly spaced intervals.

Wyatt simply watched Jenna. Her movements were different in this place. She was comfortable here, even though she was technically underground hiding from the world. It showed in the gentle, practiced way she'd handled the clay. The way her eyes had half focused on what she was doing, almost as though an instinct from within drove her more than what she could capture with her senses.

"I know why you're not saying anything. It's a terrible name." She scouted for a clear spot, then lifted the disk and the mug and set it on the third shelf, all without looking at him.

"It's not." The name fit. Somewhat fantastical, somewhat bold. It spoke of a woman who'd had the strength to do what most would find unthinkable. Even now, in the face of death, she held on, thought of others before herself, was willing to do whatever it took to bring to justice whoever wanted to see her—well, her sister—dead. "I think it's exactly right. Where did it come from?"

"I told you my mother thought of herself as a princess in a fairy tale, searching for a prince? Reality was not her friend." Jenna adjusted the coffee mug, then backed away from the cabinet. "Looks like Christa's making someone a matched set of tableware. It's all drying, waiting to be fired." She was quiet for a long time, studying the shelves.

Wyatt let her be. He still needed a minute to absorb the way she'd gifted him with her identity.

She'd trusted him with it, and he had considered betraying her trust by handing it over to authorities higher than himself. The fact they already knew had saved him from having to make the call, but he was still trapped between emotions and duty. It tightened his muscles, left him paralyzed between his job and his honor.

Jenna ran a thumb along a plate. "Anyone in town getting married any time soon?"

"Besides Erin and Jason? I have no idea." Wyatt cleared his throat, trying to get rid of whatever had stuck there. Could be admiration. Could be guilt. "Could be for them."

"Could be." When Jenna turned from the shelves, she

kept her eyes on the door. "I'm fairly certain my mom felt like her name was too normal. Constance Brady. Doesn't have a very regal quality to it, at least it never did to her. I'm not sure where she came up with Genevieve, but she always said it sounded like a fairy princess."

"It kind of does."

Flaring her nostrils, Jenna rolled her eyes to the ceiling, the effect pretty comical, considering the circumstances. "This girl is so *not* a fairy princess. It was a good day if I came home without a new hole in my clothes from climbing trees or roughhousing with the neighborhood kids."

"Somehow, you being a tomboy doesn't surprise me. How did Amy get off so easy?"

Jenna snorted and returned to the wheel. She dropped onto the stool and rested her fingers, coated gray with a thin dust of dried clay, on the edge of the wheel. Her expression held amusement, and it lit the dark room. "Amy's birth name was Amaryllis." Her smile was in full force when she lifted her head.

Wyatt grinned at her. How could he not? Her spark was contagious.

"When she turned eighteen, she had it legally changed to Amy. Said Amaryllis was too old-fashioned and no one would ever take her seriously as a personal trainer."

"And you kept Genevieve."

"I did. Nobody but my mother called me that, and sometimes Amy would when she was trying to push my buttons. Everybody called me Eve."

"Eve doesn't fit you at all."

"It really doesn't."

"It's a little too…quiet."

"You're calling me loud? Obnoxious, maybe?" She asked the question with a raised eyebrow and a spark of challenge.

The look shot straight to his heart in a bolt of lightning that almost knocked him off his seat. She was utterly gorgeous and undeniably sassy. Wyatt wrapped his fingers around the rungs of the chair and held on tight. If he didn't, he was going to lean across the clay-dusted pottery wheel and kiss her.

Whoa. Kiss Jenna Clark? Wyatt held on to the idea. The thought was brand-new yet not shocking. Somewhere at his core, he had to admit it wasn't the first time he'd ever thought it, though it was the first time he'd ever acknowledged the inclination. He shoved out of the chair and turned away from her, crossing the tiny space to the wall of shelves she'd recently abandoned.

Kissing her was out of the question. It was dangerous not only to her safety, since he was her sole protector, but also to his own sanity. They'd never work. She'd proven adept at keeping secrets and he'd never be able to know for certain if she was telling him the truth. He wouldn't risk being a fool again.

"No, Eve is definitely not me. Not now." Jenna's tone had shifted from playful to determined, causing Wyatt to turn toward her.

She shifted the wheel from side to side beneath her fingers. "I used to be a lot quieter. A lot less willing to fight for myself and for the people I loved. I guess Jenna Clark is a little different than Eve Brady."

Cutter. She was talking about the way Logan Cutter had treated her.

Wyatt balled his fists. Cutter had taken a perfectly amazing woman and tried to crush her, to beat her into submission. His jaw tightened until his head ached. If he could, he'd find a way to go back in time to El Paso before she met Logan and steer her clear. He'd—

The radio at his hip hissed static. "Movement on the south perimeter. Owens, come in from the east. Stephens, stay at your location."

Jenna was on her feet, a flicker of panic in her expression. "What's happening?"

He lifted the radio. "Ten four." Shoving it into place on his belt, he slipped his pistol from its holster and headed for the heavy door that kept Jenna safe from the outside world, but unfortunately kept him from seeing if anyone approached.

"Wyatt?"

He kept his ear tuned to the door, unwilling to look at Jenna. Unwilling to tell her the truth… Despite their best efforts, someone had found her.

Jenna breathed in, out… Too fast. Too shallow. Her body tensed as she rested her palm on the pottery wheel, seeking something solid to give her balance.

Carved out of the side of the mountain, this room had always felt cool, sheltered and safe.

Now, the walls closed in. She couldn't see out. Couldn't see if anyone approached, or how many people approached. Didn't know if it was light or dark.

She was trapped. If someone burst through the door there was nowhere to run.

Nothing stood between her and death. Nothing.

Except Wyatt.

Heart pounding, lungs screaming, legs watery, Jenna fought to control her darting gaze and forced it to rest on Wyatt.

He stood near the door, his eyes on the handle, his head cocked toward the thick wood as though he was listening for telltale sounds outside. The lines of his face were tense, his jaw tight. The expression had to be paining his raw, bruised cheek. He'd removed his pistol from his holster and held it in both hands, low before him, ready to defend her.

To defend…her. Once again, Wyatt Stephens stood between Jenna and danger. Once again, he was willing to be her first and last line of defense.

To die for her if the moment called for such a terrible, drastic choice.

Spots danced before her eyes, and Jenna sank onto the stool she'd vacated, leaning her head forward onto the pottery wheel. She had to regulate her breathing, had to get control of herself or she'd sprawl to the floor, a fainting specimen of a woman who'd done nothing but add to the burden Wyatt already carried on her behalf.

On behalf of a woman who meant nothing.

Inhale. Exhale. One. Two. Her body slowly relaxed but her ears tensed, listening for something, anything outside the door. Footsteps. Shouts. Gunshots.

More voices crackled from the radio but Jenna

couldn't make them out. They were garbled and low, as though Wyatt had turned down the volume.

"Jenna?" His voice hissed into her mind, low and insistent. "Jenna, look at me."

She tried, but her muscles wouldn't obey her brain's command.

"*Now*, Jenna!" The quiet order held all of the force of a shout.

Inhaling deeply, she pressed her hands against the cool metal wheel and forced herself upright.

Wyatt was watching her, his eyes capturing hers across the small space. "Are you okay?"

Swallowing hard, Jenna tried again to breathe normally. "Tell me what's happening." She needed to know. Nothing could be as bad as her imagination, which had painted an army of machine-gun-wielding super soldiers singularly focused on taking her out of this world.

He regarded her for a second, then divided his attention between her and the door. "Two men. One coming in from the south. He's the diversion. Another on the north side. They didn't count on us spotting them both, or on us having men in the woods watching for exactly this maneuver." He shot her a reassuring—if grim—smile. "This will be over any second."

When he tilted his head toward the door, Jenna shook her head. No. This would not be over *any second*. Wyatt, the Mountain Springs Police Department and federal agents had taken her to the outskirts of town, to a bomb shelter in the side of a mountain. And still she'd been found. Her final safe place had been destroyed. Christa's mountain retreat was no longer a sanctuary.

"Christa!" She cried out the name then clamped her hand over her mouth. With wide eyes, she tried to communicate the silent question to Wyatt. If they were safe in the bomb shelter turned art studio, where was Christa?

"She's safe," Wyatt whispered. "The minute we spotted movement, Early left the perimeter and entered the house. He moved her to an interior room."

Jenna lowered her hand, but she didn't relax. What if it wasn't enough? Once again, someone innocent was in danger because of her.

Maybe she was wrong to stay close to Mountain Springs. Maybe it really was time to pack her bags and flee. Staying was selfish. It was for her.

It was going to get someone else killed.

The radio came to life again, and Jenna shot to her feet, ready to move.

Wyatt listened, flicked a glance toward Jenna, spoke into the device before he listened again, then hooked it onto his belt and holstered his pistol. "They're in custody. It's safe."

For now. The words weren't spoken, but they hung in the air louder than if they had been.

"What now?" The answer would be to run again. She had no doubt, but she needed to hear him say it or the truth wouldn't register as reality. She'd plod on in her denial until her world was forcibly jerked out from under her. Jenna's knees wobbled.

Wyatt crossed the small space to her and his hands sought her elbows, his fingers wrapping around her arms, warm and firm. "You okay?"

Jenna kept her eyes on the shirt buttons at his chest.

The way he held her arms left her hands nowhere to rest but against his sides, right above his hips. He was solid. Safe.

She needed something safe right now.

She needed something constant.

She needed that something to be Wyatt.

Her heart hammered so loudly he had to be able to hear it. For the umpteenth time today, he'd stood between her and danger. He'd been willing to die rather than let someone get to her. He'd protected her at the possible expense of his own safety, of his own life.

No one had ever done anything even remotely like that for her before. No one had ever thought of her as valuable.

She raised her head and found him looking at her, his expression guarded. When her eyes locked in on his, something shifted in his expression. His fingers flinched at her elbows, tightening briefly. He scanned her face, then dropped his gaze to her lips, hesitating there before his eyes lifted, intense, asking a question Jenna wasn't sure she could answer.

He drew her the barest inch closer, then dipped his chin as though seeking her permission.

Permission she gave with a lift of her own chin and a tightening of her hands at his waist.

"Stephens, stay in place until we double-check the perimeter." Arch Thompson's voice squawked through the radio, slicing between them like a waterfall.

Jenna gasped, and Wyatt inhaled quickly as though something had scared him out of a deep sleep. Keeping one hand on her elbow, he reached for the radio and lifted it from his belt, his eyes never leaving hers. "Ten four."

When he reset the radio into place, he dropped his other hand and let his gaze graze her forehead, a rueful smile tipping one corner of his mouth. "You have..." He lifted his hand and ran a thumb along her forehead, the motion leaving behind a scrape of grit. His gaze shifted, and rested higher on her forehead, then he brushed her hairline.

Her scar.

Jenna dropped her hands from his waist and pulled away, her thigh colliding with the stool. He couldn't ask about the scar. She touched her forehead where his fingers had first landed, and dried clay from where she'd rested her forehead on the pottery wheel flaked off and slid down her nose. The distraction would have to work. "Well, that's not embarrassing." Sarcasm. She needed it. Because kissing him would have been a thousand times more embarrassing and a million times more painful than a smudge on her skin.

She grabbed a rag from a side table and turned away, scrubbing at the spot. Maybe he hadn't noticed she'd been about to cave in and kiss him. Maybe she'd read everything wrong and he was simply helping her stay on her feet.

Maybe she was overwrought and suffering some sort of psychological connection to a man who was willing to protect her. There was nothing else to it. There couldn't be. She was historically bad at reading cues from men, at knowing whom to trust and whom not to trust.

She was Wyatt's assignment. Nothing more. His job was the sole reason she had any value to him. He'd protect anyone the way he was protecting her. She needed to remember the truth. She also needed to remember who she was.

A loner. On her own.

Even if he thought he cared about her, it wouldn't last. Sooner or later, he'd realize she had nothing to offer and he'd find someone who could love him the way he deserved to be loved. That person wasn't her. It had never been her. It would never be her.

Tapping the wheel with two fingers, Wyatt looked at Jenna as though he was about to say something else. Finally, he turned away. "We're supposed to… To shelter in place for a while, make sure there's no second wave coming. Might as well eat."

Eat. She'd forgotten all about the burrito he'd brought, one more act of care and concern she couldn't fit into the giant puzzle piecing together their new relationship. Every time she thought she had everything figured out and found her balance, he shifted a piece and reset the whole picture. "Yeah. Sure. Okay." Her stomach revolted at the thought of food, but from past experience she knew food was important, would bolster her for what came next.

Not to mention, it would give them something to do while they waited, trapped together in what was rapidly turning into an underground prison.

They both washed their hands at the small sink in the corner, then ate in silence. Jenna racked her brain for a conversation starter, but nothing she could think of fit the situation or the mood, which had twisted the air into knots around them. It was as though neither of them knew what to make of whatever had passed between them, but couldn't figure out how to ignore it and move forward.

An hour passed with Wyatt checking his phone, and making a few comments that fell like wet clay to the floor.

Jenna picked every fleck of nail polish from one hand and was contemplating starting the other hand after another half hour passed. She glanced at the clay Christa kept wedged and ready. Maybe she could start another piece, but then Wyatt would watch and...

No. They had to talk about what had happened, or they were destined for a worse relationship when this was over than the one they'd had before. She'd grown used to Wyatt over the past day. Had watched her illusions about his personality and his heart shatter. Returning to short barbs and cold nods would cut her too much to bear.

Ignoring each other and dwelling in this awkwardness would be worse.

"Wyatt?" Her voice cracked. She cleared her throat as his head lifted. "Can we talk about—"

Pounding on the heavy wood door brought them both to their feet, Wyatt slipping his pistol from the holster as he edged to the door, holding one finger to his lips then motioning Jenna to the side of the room.

She couldn't swallow. Her mind revolted. Enough was enough. She was tired of panic. Tired of fear. Tired of...everything.

"It's Thompson." Arch's voice bled through the door.

Wyatt hesitated, then opened the door slowly, weapon at the ready as though he didn't trust his own ears.

Chief Thompson walked into the room wearing a totally incongruous grin. He looked at Wyatt, then at Jenna, who stood to the side, too numb to wonder at his expression. "I heard from Agent Nance. One of the men we apprehended tonight started talking in the back seat of the car before they could even interrogate him, spilling intel like his life depended on it." His smile widened. "Long story short, it's over. Jenna, you're safe."

NINE

Wyatt scrubbed eyes scratchy from yet another sleepless night. They'd all spent a restless night trying to sleep in various rooms at the station until the chief had released Jenna to return to work with Wyatt in tow. Although the chief viewed it as a mere precaution and that Jenna was likely safe, Wyatt didn't believe the evidence. Not for one second. He'd heard the same before and it had proven false.

Jenna wasn't out of danger. It didn't matter what the Feds said. It didn't matter what their suspects said. This felt like déjà vu all over again, right to the uneasy dread in his gut, the warning that something bad was coming.

Wyatt leaned a hip against the desk in Jenna's office and stared out the two-way mirror into the storefront area. Four rows of four easels faced the side wall, where Liza demonstrated a painting of a stylized sunrise over a mountain. A group of seven men, women and children followed her every move with mixed results, though everyone seemed to be having fun.

None of them paid any sort of special attention to

Jenna, who maintained her spot at the coffee bar. She'd alternated the day between serving customers, cleaning and simply staring out the front window.

Staring anywhere but in his direction, if he was telling the truth.

She hadn't said more than two sentences to him since he'd followed her into the shop early in the morning. "Stay in the office" and "don't scare the customers" didn't really qualify as conversation. It could be she was upset with him for talking Chief Thompson into extending his guard duty for a few more days. She hadn't seemed to appreciate his presence, almost seemed to resent it, in fact.

He couldn't blame her. He'd overheard her on the phone with Erin in the small hours of the night. She wanted this to be over. Wyatt's continued presence did nothing but reinforce the fact she might still have something to be afraid of.

He couldn't believe the federal team had backed off so quickly, taking their suspect at his word. It was foolish to trust a criminal. Even Chief Thompson had been a bit cagey this morning, refusing to meet Wyatt's eye.

There was a bigger issue at play, one nobody wanted to discuss, and Wyatt couldn't figure out what it was. The men arrested at Christa's had confessed to coming after Jenna, but they claimed they were lone wolves out to get revenge on Amy for taking down Grant Meyer.

Their confession didn't feel right. The whole thing was too easy and the entire situation made his head hurt. He'd have to talk with the chief later, try to find out what was really happening behind the scenes. It

would have to be at a time when Jenna was safely somewhere out of earshot, though. Getting her worked up
again wasn't something he wanted to do. The woman
needed peace badly. Seemed she also needed time away
from him, which she wasn't getting until he knew for
certain this had all blown over and she was truly safe.

There was one other reason Jenna might be avoiding him, one he wished he could avoid himself. Wyatt
pinched the bridge of his nose and shut his eyes, wishing
there was a way to kick himself hard enough to knock
some sense into his own head.

He'd almost kissed her last night, and the moment
hadn't left him alone since. He'd lain awake on the
couch in Chief Thompson's office, undeniably aware she
was down the hall in the break room, wishing he could
stand, march in there and tell her how she'd wrecked
him.

But he could never confess any of those things.

Because she couldn't wreck him.

Not only were every one of his thoughts dangerous
and unprofessional, but they were also downright stupid
in light of his knotted feelings for the woman who stood
a thin wall and a couple dozen feet away from him, but
who might as well have taken up residence on Jupiter.

He'd completely lost his mind last night. The things
she'd shared with him. The way she'd looked so terrified and vulnerable when the warning came to tell them
she'd been found.

The way she'd looked at him with complete trust,
total faith, and something entirely too gooey and warm.

He'd practically dragged her into his arms, relieved she was safe, half-scared she wasn't.

No woman had ever looked at him the way Jenna had in Christa Naylor's old fallout shelter, standing there with her hands at his waist. He could still feel them, couldn't seem to scratch away the sensation. Her touch had felt...normal. Right. As though she'd rested her hands right there a thousand times before and would do so a thousand times again.

Her look. It had made him feel...things. Warm fuzzy things, where his heart used to be. Wyatt shuddered and scrubbed the top of his head. Not even Kari had made him feel so completely like a superhero, as though he could do anything, could scale a rock face without a rope, could stand up to a hundred armed men with nothing but a pocketknife.

Brother. He sounded like one of those TV romance movies Erin had on half of the time.

And romance this was not.

The mere thought of Kari froze his emotions into cold mountain river rocks. She'd lied to him and he'd bought it. She'd been using him, and it had almost cost him everything.

Lies. Jenna had been living lies for three years. Even now, with all she'd told him, there were pieces of herself she was holding back. He could never trust she'd confessed everything. In the back of his mind he would know she was accomplished at being someone different than she was. He'd always wonder if she was telling the truth, if he could trust her words.

He could definitely never trust she wouldn't lie to

him the same way Kari had. He'd missed the signs then, so it was completely conceivable he could miss them all again.

Motion on the other side of the window put the screeching brakes on an oncoming pity train. Members of the class were gathering their canvases, chatting with one another and with Liza, or grabbing a final coffee creation from Jenna.

Once again, he'd let his emotions take over his mind and he'd missed everything happening in the main room. Further proof he needed to keep his thoughts in line.

Wyatt glanced at his watch. It was almost closing time, later than he'd thought. With more bluegrass concerts tonight at the Fine Arts Center, the activity in town would crank into high gear soon. He'd like to get Jenna to her apartment before the streets crowded with even more tourists.

When the shop cleared out, Liza started collecting brushes from the middle row of easels, but Jenna stopped her at the end of the row and took the brushes from her hand. Their voices were a low murmur drifting along the short hallway, but he couldn't make out any words. After a short conversation that involved Jenna gesturing toward the door quite a bit, Liza hugged her then practically skipped out, Jenna locking the door behind her.

Wyatt checked the time on his phone. A few minutes before six. She'd probably sent Liza home to get ready for a date with—

"We need to talk." Jenna's voice from the doorway

came out of nowhere, jerking his head around so fast it pained his neck.

Uh-oh. Wyatt straightened. How had she managed to sneak up on him? And why did her voice send his heartbeat to the same jolt he'd felt standing with her in Christa's bomb shelter twenty-four hours earlier? He had to check himself, to gain full control before he could turn to look at her.

Jenna stood in the office doorway, one hand hanging at her side, one fiddling with the simple silver flower pendant she wore at her throat. Her jaw was set, as though whatever she had to say, she was determined to say it. Likely, she was finding her footing after the whiplash of the past few days and was about to lay into him for being here, shadowing her when the chief had assured her they had the all clear.

Except she didn't look very bold. She looked…lost. Uncertain.

Every rational thought he'd been thinking, every reason he should keep his professional mask on and pretend he didn't notice her, evaporated. He was in trouble.

Wyatt pocketed his phone, then shoved his hands into his pockets to keep from reaching for her. He couldn't. He wouldn't. "Okay. We can talk. What's going on?" Every man in the world knew "we need to talk" could lead to trouble, but here he went, stepping right into it.

With a nod, Jenna dropped her hand to her side and stiffened as though she was steeling herself for whatever she had to say. Her auburn hair slipped across her shoulder to her back, leaving a clear view of the tight determination in her jaw. "It's about what happened at Christa's."

His mind raced to the exact spot he'd been fighting to keep it away from all day—the moment when something bigger had clicked between them, when she'd changed everything about him.

But it was impossible she was here to discuss those few short moments. There was no way she'd been obsessing about those brief flickers all day the way he had. Not after the way she'd backed off and acted supremely uncomfortable in his presence afterward. Not after the way she'd ignored him since they'd walked into the building this morning. "If this is about how those men found you, we're working on finding out—"

"No." Jenna stayed in the doorway.

Crossing his arms over his chest, Wyatt faced her head-on as he leaned against the edge of her desk. Though she hadn't stepped into the room, the small square footage in the office meant she was only a few feet away, close enough to hear her breathing.

Close enough to reach out and tug her to him.

Seriously. This heart thing was getting out of control. He needed to focus. Now. "Okay, what's bothering you about it?"

She studied him for a long time, then she dropped her gaze to the ground somewhere around his feet, the determined look she'd worn seconds before slipping into some kind of sadness he couldn't quite read. "Nothing. I've got… It's nothing." She waved a hand as though dismissing him, then backed into the hallway and turned toward the front room. "I have to… I have to clean the shop so we can close for the day. You have to go home tonight. Get some real sleep. Accept all of this is over."

The way she said it, the drop in her voice, the slope of her shoulders… She wasn't talking about the threat to her life. She was talking about them and the tenuous friendship that had replaced their typical growling. The closeness they'd formed out of necessity.

She wasn't relieving him of duty. She was kicking his friendship to the curb.

"No." Okay, now his mouth was out of control, too. But when she froze in place, one eyebrow raised in question, Wyatt knew he wouldn't take back the word for anything.

He refused to return to hostility or even to indifference. It wasn't in his nature to be at odds with anyone, and he'd been at odds with Jenna for too long. Now that he'd been allowed to see beneath the surface, to understand even the smallest bit of who she was… Now that she'd trusted him with her real identity… He couldn't do it. He could never look at her with the same nonchalance he had in the past. It was impossible. "No. This isn't over."

"Wyatt, they caught the guys. They confessed. They're at whatever interrogation room they're at singing like canaries or whatever it is you law people say."

The laugh he swallowed almost choked him. "Not that. We honestly never say that."

"Well…" His amusement clearly irritated her. "Either way—"

"You can stop with the act. You know I'm not talking

about the danger to your life." Even though he didn't believe she was safe now, either.

Her expression shifted, the tight lines around her mouth and above her eyes softening. "It has to be over. It can't be anything else. It can't be anything…more."

Wyatt rose from the edge of her desk. So her head really *had* been in the same place as his all day.

The wrong place.

Or was it the exact right place?

Emotion overran reason. He needed her. Needed the way she made him feel twenty feet tall, like the hero of her story. Even more, he needed to *be* the hero of her story. Her whole life, no one had protected her, everyone had walked out on her.

He refused to be another in a long line to abandon her. He wanted to be the one who stayed, who shielded her from any person who ever dared try to hurt her again.

Before she could tuck into herself and run, Wyatt reached out. He stopped short of touching her, though. She'd ignore him or, worse, turn away. Instead, he extended his hand, palm up.

An invitation.

TEN

Jenna stared at Wyatt's outstretched hand. He didn't move. Didn't waver. Simply waited...for her.

She froze.

This was her office. Her shop. Her normal, everyday, unimportant life...until a couple of days ago, at least.

But here was Wyatt in the midst of it. Not normal, everyday, or unimportant. And this wasn't an invitation to take his hand.

It was an invitation to change everything.

He couldn't possibly mean it, not in the way her heart wanted him to. He didn't know who she really was. Didn't know the thoughts running through her head. Didn't know she had nothing to offer him.

He was incredible, wonderful, perfect. She was a wreck in every possible way.

Still, everything in her cried out for him. It would feel good to be loved, to be needed, to share everyday life with Wyatt Stephens.

She lifted her hand and inhaled deeply, the breath catching in her throat as a familiar odor wafted in.

Gasoline.

"Wyatt..."

His hand fell to his side as his expression shifted from soft and questioning to firm and determined, the same look he'd worn each time he'd put himself between her and danger. He grabbed her arm, shifting her behind him as he reached for his cell phone. "Probably nothing, but I'm going to—"

Glass shattered at the front of the building. A light flashed, then grew steadily brighter in the shop.

Jenna whipped toward the light. Flames spread rapidly along the center of the room, hungrily licking the tile floor, feeding off the breeze from the broken front window. Voices from outside shouted and yelled, becoming muted as the sound of fire grew louder.

Wyatt shoved his phone into his pocket and reached for her hand. "We have to get out of here. Now." He dragged her out of the office and along the short hallway to the back door, but when he looked up, he halted. Expression grim, he placed his palm on the door, then jerked it away.

Jenna followed his gaze to the small screen in the corner above the door. The monitor painted a horrifying picture of the steps, one filled with thick smoke and angry flames.

There was nowhere to run. With solid brick walls on one side of the building and two layers of brick between her shop and the gallery next door, they were trapped.

He flipped the dead bolt to unlock the door, then tugged her hand and led her to the front of the shop. Although the fire ran along the floor toward the center of the room, space remained to squeeze by along the wall. Barely. They'd have to move fast.

Jenna tried to blast past Wyatt, but he tightened his grip on her hand, raising his voice to be heard over the increasing pop and roar of the fire. "The door."

The front door and windows burned higher and hotter than the rest of the room, nearly obliterated by the flames.

"Accelerant. Someone wanted our escape routes cut off." Wyatt dragged her backward into the office and shut the door behind them, holding his phone to his ear as he looked around the room. "Find anything. Anything you can to shove under the door. Fast."

Jenna's heart raced. He'd dragged her to the center of the building. No exits. No way out. Fire on either side of them. After all she'd been through, she was going to die today in a way her worst nightmares had never even dared to imagine, in a blaze of pain at the hands of an unseen enemy.

The roaring in her ears grew louder than the roar of the fire. Wyatt's voice, low and steady, crept through the noise. He was on the phone with Dispatch, giving their location, their situation.

Surely 911 was being inundated with calls other than Wyatt's, but would help arrive in time?

Jenna turned toward the two-way mirror and stared out into her shop. Smoke rolled to the ceiling and down along the walls in sickening waves. Fire licked at easels, canvases. Flames sought what they could consume and went to work, slowly devouring her life. Her work. Her life.

"Jenna!" Wyatt's bark jerked her out of her panic. "The door. Get something under the door. Now!"

She scanned the room, eyes lighting on a new box of aprons the post office had delivered two days earlier, still waiting to be embroidered with the shop's logo.

The shop was rapidly burning into oblivion as she stood helpless to stop it.

She'd already lost everything. How much more could they take from her? Her chest and throat aching, Jenna pried open the box and shoved the material between the floor and the bottom of the door, praying, praying, praying. *Lord, please. Please get us out of this. Please.*

She stood and backed away from the door, staring at the floor, waiting for the smoke to consume them. They'd die from smoke inhalation before the fire ever reached them, a blessing and a curse.

She should have taken Wyatt's hand earlier instead of leaving him standing there, his heart in his palm. When he offered his hand to her, she should have risked it, should have taken the chance. She would have…had she known it was the last thing she'd ever do.

If they survived this, she would… Unless he'd changed his mind.

A strong arm wrapped around her waist, holding her against an even stronger chest as Wyatt turned her away from the door, once again putting himself closest to the threat. He was silent, though he still held the phone to his ear and the dispatcher's words leaked through the speaker, too low to be discernible, but solid and soothing nonetheless.

Wyatt tipped his head forward, his lips brushing her

ear, the low whisper warm against her skin. "Fire department's already dispatched. They're a couple of minutes away. We'll get through this. Hang on."

Jenna nodded once. The room was growing hotter. Outside, red-tinged smoke completely filled the front room. It wouldn't be long before the heat shattered the mirror standing as the last line of defense between them and the flames. Once the mirror was gone, the smoke would overtake them and it would be too late.

It might already be too late. Mountain Springs had a volunteer fire department with only one full-time firefighter on duty at any given time. Assembling the firefighters could take a while.

"It only takes one truck and one hose to get us out of here." It was as though Wyatt had read her thoughts. His arm around her waist tightened, and he laid his cheek against the back of her head. "We're going to get out of here. I promise."

It was a vow he couldn't possibly keep. Somehow, though, it leaked peace into her muscles, relaxed her against his chest. *Lord, let it be true. Let help get here in time.*

But if they didn't. If today was the day she truly lost everything but her salvation…

Sweat trickled down her spine as the room heated even more, as the fire popped and cracked and roared louder than ever in the front room, drowning out all of her senses.

Wyatt's chest moved, his breathing hard. He had to be as terrified as she was, but he never let it show.

And he never let her go.

All she had to do was turn her head a few inches, meet him where he'd invited her last night and again this evening. Into a kiss, a moment that would pour out the feelings she was desperately trying to unravel before everything was gone.

Her ears roared with a combination of her heartbeat and the fire and a new sound, a whine that rose and fell as it grew closer…

Sirens.

Wyatt relaxed, letting his cheek slide next to hers. "We're going to make it. I unlocked the door so they could get in." His lips brushed her hair, his voice low and husky as the smell of smoke intensified. "Hang on."

Her eyes slipped closed. Her head turned toward him. She should say something. Tell him—

A crash jerked her into reality. Wyatt's arm slipped from her waist and he whipped around toward the office door, one hand reaching behind him to find hers.

The office door burst open and a firefighter pushed through with a cloud of smoke, gear hiding the face although the eyes were familiar…

Erin.

Jenna nearly wilted at the sight of Wyatt's cousin and her best friend. Wyatt's hand was the sole thing giving her strength as Erin moved aside and aimed a finger out the door. "Fire at the rear's out. Let's go."

Wyatt led the way, tugging Jenna with him, Erin bringing up the rear as the window in the office exploded.

Jenna hesitated. Her life. She was leaving everything she had left of her life behind.

Wyatt urged her forward and shouted over his shoulder, "Don't look back, Jen. Keep moving. Trust me."

She stumbled out the door behind Wyatt, gulping fresh air until he drew her into his arms and held her head against his chest, his heart pounding against her ear. *Don't look back.*

Staring at the floor, Jenna let the tears leak out. Everything was gone. Everything.

Trust in Wyatt might be the only thing she had left.

Wyatt stood at the front window of Jenna's apartment and stared up the street. Red and white fire engine lights cut through the thick black smoke roiling from the building where her livelihood, her joy, had been. The fire was mostly out, but the lights flashed on as firefighters searched for hot spots and doused what was left of the flames.

Gripping the window ledge, Wyatt scanned the street below. Officer Mike Owens had pulled his cruiser as close as possible to the stairs leading to Jenna's apartment, and he stood guard over the entrance, moving aside to let Officers Isaac Hayes and Brian Early make their way up the stairs. They probably had news. Three more officers and two federal agents had stationed themselves around the block, keeping an eye on the building and on the bystanders taking in the excitement at Jenna's shop.

Behind him at the window in the small living room, Alex "Rich" Richardson stood vigil, watching the alley below. A battle buddy of Erin's fiancé, Jason, Rich had arrived at the shop while they were still being checked out by paramedics. A close friend and a Special Forces soldier who'd done more than his share of tours overseas—there was no one else Wyatt would rather have partnered with him in this moment.

Wyatt reached over and unlocked the door, then opened it for Early and Hayes, who slipped in and shut it behind them. If Chief Thompson had withdrawn them from the perimeter and sent them in person, it must have been important. "What's going on?"

Early surveyed the apartment, a grim look darkening his expression. He wouldn't meet Wyatt's eyes but looked to Hayes to deliver whatever blow was coming.

Hayes took the lead. "Chief sent me to let you know to watch what you say on the radio or the phones. The federal team is concerned about communications being compromised after they found Jenna at Christa's."

Wyatt drummed his fingers on his thigh. "They think we've been tapped? What are the odds somebody tailed us out there?"

"Pretty low."

Great. Now communications were possibly compromised. Someone was coming after Jenna with some serious firepower. The possibilities kept getting bigger. They had four men in custody already. How big was this crew? And who did they work for?

"How soon before we move again?" Early finally spoke. "The chief and the federal team are both getting antsy with Jenna out in the open and so close to the action."

"When we move is their call." If the decision was Wyatt's to make, they'd already be gone. "There's too much chaos downstairs now to try to get her out of here. It would be too easy for someone to slip in and follow us or, worse, make a move in the middle of the crowd." After today, it was clear that collateral damage wasn't an issue to whoever was trying to get to Jenna.

Early nodded. "Understandable." He elbowed Hayes and aimed a finger at the door. "We're out. We have to get to our posts but we'll check in again."

When they let themselves out, Wyatt locked the door then surveyed the crowds on the street, pausing on each and every person clogging the sidewalk by the barriers erected to protect the firefighters as the blaze was brought into submission. One of them was likely the torch who'd started the whole thing. Arsonists tended to enjoy watching their work.

Chief Thompson had been texting information to Wyatt, though he'd likely stop now that the federal team was suspicious of their tech. The chief had kept Wyatt apprised of what they learned as they learned it. So far, all of their information amounted to a huge bag of nothing. A handful of eyewitnesses reported seeing a man in jeans and a dark green or black hoodie heft something through the front window seconds before the fire started. He'd darted around the corner, likely where he had a getaway car stashed.

Wyatt had known Jenna was still in danger. No one had listened.

Now Jenna was in her room with Erin, who'd arrived per Chief Thompson's request after the fire had been largely contained. The Feds had deemed this the quickest place to safely stash Jenna while the crowds gath-

ered below. It was close and relatively easy to defend…
as long as no one set it on fire.

Erin had brought the news that the brick exterior of
the building had withstood the fire, but the inside was
a disaster. Since she'd arrived, she'd been with Jenna,
offering comfort Wyatt couldn't and shouldn't be trying to dish out himself. "I messed up."

"Messed up how?"

He'd forgotten Rich was in the room. He glanced over
his shoulder, but Rich was still watching the window,
not looking at him. Wyatt returned to his perusal of the
crowd, guilt driving him to search for the man who'd
tried to take both of them out this evening. "I should
have been watching."

"From what I understand, you were."

"Not well enough." Obviously. He'd been too wor-
ried about staying out of Jenna's way… Too focused
on his feelings and the way he'd nearly kissed her the
night before… He hadn't been doing his job. Instead
of hiding out in her office trying to prevent her from
being uncomfortable, he should have been on the move,
checking the perimeter of the building, keeping a closer
eye on the street. He should have been visible. Should
have insisted to Chief Thompson and Agent Nance that
his gut was right and they needed more eyes on Jenna.

Better yet, he should have insisted Jenna move to
a safe house somewhere out of town, even though she
would have fought it. If he had, the incident at her shop
never would have happened. "I let someone start a fire
literally a dozen feet away from me outside her door. I
missed the guy coming at us from the front because I

was too focused on…" Focused on Jenna. He'd been focused on her. On the way her auburn hair waved to her shoulders. On the way her green eyes were looking at him in her office and on the memory of the way they'd looked at him the night before. On how she made him feel. On too many things other than keeping her safe.

Behind him, Rich heaved a loud breath and kept his silence for all of thirty seconds. "You care about her." His voice was deep, a low rumble punctuating the words.

Wyatt didn't answer. He didn't have to. His silence would say more than enough.

"Take yourself off of her case, Stephens. If you care anything about her at all, back off."

Wyatt's head jerked at the ferocity of Rich's tone. He pivoted on one heel to stare at his friend, who never turned his attention from his surveillance of the alley below. All he got was a full view of the back of Rich's military-short dark hair.

Back off from protecting Jenna? Let someone else be by her side 24/7? It would kill him. He wouldn't be able to sleep wondering if she was okay. He'd constantly be radioing whoever had the detail, checking on her. Who would he trust enough to let them watch her? Who could do it better than him?

After today, it was clear the answer to the question was "any other person on the planet."

Still, he couldn't leave her. Not now. Not when he'd made a promise to protect her. "I can't leave her."

Rich nodded, his jaw tight, a grim understanding passing between them. "Then you have to forget everything you feel for her. Swallow it. Kill it. Let it die."

Wyatt's eyes turned toward the rear of the small apartment, where Jenna remained behind closed doors with Erin. He'd thought the same thing himself, but to hear it so bluntly from someone else...

"If you don't come at this with your head fully in the game, you'll regret it for the rest of your life." Rich's tone was low, heavy with grief, and it tugged at Wyatt's soul.

This wasn't about Jenna. It was about Amber. A handful of days after Rich and Amber Ransom had announced their engagement, she was dead, murdered by a vindictive spouse who blamed Rich and Jason's team for the death of her husband overseas. The same woman who had nearly succeeded in her attempts to kill Erin. "You did what you could for her, Rich."

"I was cocky, like you are right now. I thought I was the only one who could protect her, so I didn't make her go into hiding. I didn't trust anyone else. I didn't take her onto post and let more people help. I was her fiancé. I was supposed to be the one to protect her for the rest of her life. I failed her. She's dead because I failed her." Before Wyatt could argue, Rich spun and caught his gaze with a fierce gray-eyed look burning with anger and grief. "Don't be so busy trying to be Jenna's hero and protector that you miss something and let her get killed."

Wyatt couldn't even blink. Rich's pain rooted him to the floor, his head spinning with options, with truth, with decisions.

The door to Jenna's bedroom opened and Erin exited with Jenna right behind her. Her auburn hair was dark, damp from a recent shower. With her face scrubbed free of what little makeup she normally wore and her eyes rimmed pink with tears, she was more vulnerable than Wyatt had ever seen her. He wanted to turn his back completely on the window he was supposed to be monitoring and stride across the space between them, pull her against him the way he had at the store and let her heart beat against his, reassurance they were both still alive.

He had taken two steps toward her, lost in the need to be next to her, when he felt Rich watching him.

One look at Rich's expression, torn in fresh grief even all these months later, stopped Wyatt where he stood, freezing his feet to the floor.

The truth had never been clearer. He either had to step away from Jenna physically and let someone else be her defender…or he had to rip his heart away from her.

Either way, the decision he was about to make could destroy them both.

ELEVEN

Jenna wrapped her fingers around the warm coffee mug Erin had filled and leaned forward, resting her forearms on the granite counter in her kitchen. The column standing at the end of the bar to separate the kitchen from the living area was wide enough to block the front window and the lights alternating red and white in the glass, a vivid reminder of everything she had lost.

It was also wide enough to keep Wyatt from her sight.

She needed to get out of this apartment. After the invasion a couple of nights ago, her home no longer felt safe. It had been violated. Her store had been torched. Wyatt stood silent guard at her front window, while another man she'd met only a few times before stood watch over the alley. She no longer had the luxury of curling into a ball and shutting out the world—to "turtle" as Amy had once called it—because the world had ripped off her shell.

There had to be a place she could run, somewhere she could settle in and feel safe again.

For a few minutes earlier today, she'd thought her safe place would be wherever Wyatt was.

Jenna pressed her fingers tighter against the ceramic mug, running her thumb along a ridge in the glaze. For almost an hour, she'd taken refuge in her bedroom, muffling sobs she didn't want to pour out into her pillow, alternately praying no one would hear and hoping Wyatt would come in to comfort her and hold her the way he had before.

After Erin and her fellow firefighters had led Wyatt and Jenna a safe distance away from the building, the paramedics had checked them both out, suggesting they go to the hospital to make sure there had been no smoke inhalation. Both she and Wyatt had declined. She wouldn't feel safe there. He insisted she needed to be somewhere sheltered. But the entire time he'd been beside her, his hand wrapped around hers, supporting her, saying things silently that neither of them could say out loud. Not yet.

The grip on her hand had felt like a silent promise, a continuation of what had begun before the fire tore them apart.

But he hadn't come for her as she'd cried. She needed Wyatt. After a shower to wash the smoke from her hair and skin, she'd finally found the courage to seek him out. And he'd almost come to her. Almost.

Then he'd hesitated, had had a silent conversation across the room with Jason's friend Rich...

And he'd turned away. Slowly. Deliberately. Back to the window and the street below without even saying a word.

It had been half an hour since he shut her out. Erin had since returned to the scene of the fire to oversee the start of cleanup.

Life would be easier if they'd all leave. Jenna's head felt like it was going to explode. She needed her hiking boots and a tent, a trek to the high country, something...

Whatever had happened last night at Christa's or today in her shop when Wyatt had extended his hand, asking her for something she still couldn't quite decipher, was dead now.

She'd been right all along. He had a job to do. The emotions that had tilted her world had been nothing more than a vanishing moment for him.

Why should Wyatt be different than every man who'd come and gone from her mother's life? She was the same Genevieve Brady. She could change her name, but she couldn't change who she fundamentally was. Something in her repelled everyone around her, including her own mother, who had never been able to stand by her daughters for more than a few weeks at a time before she needed to run off and find love and excitement somewhere else.

A rustle from near the front door broke off her pity party.

Rich backed away from the window overlooking the alley and twisted his head to one side, then to the other. He checked the holster at his side and glanced at Jenna before he turned to Wyatt. "I'm going to go outside, check with the guys on the perimeter, see if I can get a word in with Erin or someone on her crew, see what they know. I'll be back in a few." He opened the door and was halfway out when he looked over his shoulder in Wyatt's direction. "You know what needs to be done."

When the door shut behind him, Jenna leaned forward slightly, bracing herself for a peek at Wyatt. He still stood at the window looking at the street, but the line of his shoulders was a wall, his neck muscles corded with a tension that expressed his emotions quite clearly.

He'd turned his back on her—literally and figuratively—but she couldn't turn hers on him. He might not care about her, but she couldn't turn off or ignore what she felt for him. Letting go of her mug, she pushed away from the counter and poured him a cup of coffee from the carafe Shelley had sent from her shop downstairs, then grabbed her own coffee and padded across the room. She kept her eyes on the burden she carried, averted from the window. She didn't want to see the destruction, wanted to pretend her dreams still stood the way they were painted in her mind, pristine and unmarred by reality. Tomorrow would come soon enough, and then she'd have to face the carnage and look to the future. Tonight, she couldn't acknowledge there might not be a future to look toward.

Careful not to touch Wyatt, she reached around him and set the mug on the wide windowsill in front of him.

He glanced at her offering. "Thanks."

Jenna hesitated. A few hours ago, she might have rested her hand on his shoulder, let him know she was there for him. Now?

Now she had to remember who she was and why there could never be anything between them. Between her and anybody. *Thanks for the reminder, God. You meant for me to do this on my own.* At this point, maybe God was tired of her and had quit listening. It would explain why her world was burning around her.

Backing off, Jenna sat on the end of the couch far-thest from Wyatt, drawing her feet beneath her and star-ing at the painting above the mantel. Again. She was living in *Groundhog Day*. "Is this how it's going to be?"

She didn't have to look at Wyatt to know he'd tensed impossibly more. It was an almost palpable motion that tightened the air in the entire apartment. "How what's going to be?" His voice stretched across the words until they almost snapped.

"Somebody always watching. Me always hiding. Never having a life unless I run. And even then, al-ways looking over my shoulder."

"We're going to end this. I made you a promise."

"You know you can't keep it."

Everything froze. It was almost as if time stopped and solidified Wyatt into a statue. He didn't even breathe. When he did, it was shallow, almost.

"They're going to keep coming at me. Over and over. Until they win. You take care of one, there's going to be more. You find one, another will—"

"I get it. I'm a failure. You don't have to drive it home." He bit off the words like a bitter pill he had to swallow.

"I never said you were a failure."

"You didn't have to." He never turned, but in the reflection of the window, she could see he was watch-ing her and not the street. "The man bursting into your apartment and holding a gun on you? My fault. You nearly getting shot? My fault. The fire today? My—"

"How can you say the blame for any of those things falls on you?" He couldn't take responsibility for what evil men were doing. They were after her, not him. All he'd done was put himself in the line of fire to protect her.

"I can say it because it's true. I was slow to act. And not for the first time. It's exactly like the time I let…" He braced his hands on either side of the window and stared toward her shop, seeing things she couldn't. "Never mind. It is what it is. I can't do this with you."

Dread slicked along her throat and pooled in her stomach, turning her few sips of coffee into ice. "You can't do what?" She set her mug on the table and stood, hands shaking. "You're backing off, turning me over to someone else."

"No."

"Then what is it you can't do?" He was talking in circles, giant riddles she couldn't solve. On top of everything else swirling in her mind, she didn't need him adding to the confusion. Not that he hadn't already. Now he was putting it into ever more circuitous words.

His fingers tightened on the window frame, and he kept his eyes on the outside. "You can't stay here, you know."

Fine. He wasn't going to answer. Fine. Fine. Fine. She didn't deserve to know anyway. All she'd done was put him in danger. If she really cared about him, she'd ask for someone else, would let him off the hook.

But fear kept her from asking Wyatt to leave. She didn't really know any of the other officers very well. She definitely didn't trust the federal agents outside. She'd met them only once and they were entirely too by the book for her. The way she'd once thought Wyatt was. If her world was going to rock again and she was going to have to leave the safety of everything she knew, she wanted something solid with her for as far as she could carry it. She wanted Wyatt, even if he was rejecting her as hard as he could.

Sinking onto the couch, she reached for her mug and cradled it in her hands. She couldn't make herself take a sip. Her stomach would surely revolt, but she needed the warmth in her hands, the reminder she'd once had a sister who'd loved her…until Jenna had shoved her away.

The handmade clock she'd bought from Larissa Nielsen ticked off more seconds than she cared to count before Wyatt pulled his phone from his pocket and read the screen. "Chief Thompson's coming. He's got Agent Nance with him." He finally looked over his shoulder at her, finally met her eyes.

And his expression told her the news they brought with them would not be good.

Jenna was killing him.

Wyatt braced one hand on the window frame and scrubbed the other along his jaw, scraping a couple of days' worth of beard. No, it wasn't fair to blame this on her. The situation was killing him.

His muscles physically ached with the need to walk across the room, sit on the couch next to Jenna and shield her. No words, just presence. No need to talk about how much pain twisted in his chest over not being able to hold her.

Rich's footsteps on the stairs reinforced the common sense he'd laid on Wyatt earlier. Distance. Distance was the only way to keep her safe. Not that it was doing him any good. He was focused more on trying not to think of her than he was when he was thinking of her.

Whatever that meant.

He unlocked the door, then returned to his station as Rich entered, followed by the chief and Agent Nance.

When the door was firmly closed behind him, Chief Thompson broke the silence. "You can stand down, Wyatt. I've got enough men downstairs, and this conversation involves you."

Wyatt's eyebrows drew together, and he turned from the window, wary about letting his guard slip. He'd been Jenna's primary protector from the start. Were they about to relieve him of this duty now?

She was watching him from her perch on the edge of the couch. As strong as he knew she was, it was clear to anyone this was taking a toll. The lines around her eyes were deep. Her mouth was tight. And she was looking straight at Wyatt with a gaze filled with uncertainty and pain.

Pain he'd caused by jerking her emotions back and forth.

He glanced at Rich. The man was right. His emotions were going to keep him from effectively protecting Jenna.

But Rich was also wrong. It was too late to squelch his feelings now. They were already firmly in place, and they were going to affect him no matter what. Nothing was going to make him back off and let someone else watch over her. His emotions were the very thing that would make him take twice as many precautions as a man who cared nothing for her.

He couldn't tell her any of those things, not while things were so far out of his control, but he also couldn't leave her to stand on her own.

Securing his pistol in its holster, he edged around Agent Nance and settled onto the couch beside Jenna, not touching her but close enough to offer his support. From the steel in the agent's gaze, she was going to need it.

The federal agent was looking at Jenna as though she was the guilty party. It was all Wyatt could do not to reach over and take her hand.

Even Chief Thompson's expression was grim as he settled into a side chair, watching Jenna and Wyatt.

Agent Nance stayed standing, though he backed up to lean against the fireplace. "I assume you'd like us to continue calling you Ms. Clark?"

They knew who she really was. Wyatt's heart ached for her.

Jenna lifted her head, her expression guarded. "Yes."

"I believe Chief Thompson told you earlier your sister's car accident was no accident."

"He did." Her voice was thin, weaker than the water she poured into her coffeepot every day. They had to end this soon, or Jenna might crumble. *Please, Lord, don't let there be any more blows coming her way.*

"We have several issues at play here." Agent Nance tugged his phone from a holster on his hip and ran his thumb along the screen before turning to Wyatt. "Officer Stephens, you played a major role in the investigation of the truck found on Overton Road?"

"Yes." This was heading in a direction he didn't want to go. If they were tying Amy's death to the truck they'd found, that could only mean—

"We have a problem." Chief Thompson sat forward in the chair and braced his elbows on his knees, eyes intent on Jenna, then on Wyatt. "Agent Nance has been briefing me on their investigation into the men who murdered Jenna's sister."

"Grant Meyer." She whispered the name, but it was loud enough for everyone in the room to hear.

The chief motioned for Agent Nance to take the other chair across from the couch.

Nance hesitated, then took a seat, never breaking his attention from Jenna. "Grant Meyer went into the wind after your sister's murder."

Jenna flinched, but no one acted as if they noticed. Wyatt laid a hand on her shoulder. This guy could really use a little more tact. He bit the inside of his lip. Now he could see why Jenna nearly ripped him apart when he'd been delivering horrible news to Erin a few months earlier.

"Meyer had quite the empire in Texas. He'd engineered a Texas circuit to move people around the state. Some of his employees were in debt bondage. He shipped them over from Mexico and multiple countries in South America, then forced them to work off the debt in his businesses. Did you know any of this?"

"No."

"What did you know about Logan Cutter's involvement?"

Jenna's mouth opened, then closed, nothing more than a small squeak escaping. She looked at Wyatt, seeming to seek support, before she swallowed and her voice returned, stronger this time. "Nothing about his involvement with Grant Meyer until I was told of it yesterday. Right before I… Before I ran from him, I found out…" She looked at Wyatt again, ran her tongue across her top lip, then stared at the floor. The silence in the room hung heavy. It was clear Nance was going to wait until she said it. "He was buying women."

"And you had no idea?"

"None." The pain in her eyes was enough to undo every man in the room. Even Chief Thompson, who worked hard to temper the compassion lying close to the surface, looked wounded.

Agent Nance appeared to be unaffected. He sat in the chair, watching Jenna with a look that bordered on disinterest.

But Wyatt recognized it. Underneath the bored expression he was searching, waiting for her to give him something only he knew he was looking for.

And he'd do whatever it took to get it.

Wyatt wanted to punch him in the nose.

As a law-enforcement officer, he understood, but his understanding didn't stop him from wanting to put an end to this. He shifted, but a quick look from the chief settled him. *Let this play out. Don't interfere.*

It was killing him.

Agent Nance glanced at his phone. "Logan Cutter

was murdered in his home two days before he was supposed to testify against Grant Meyer. He'd made a deal to reduce his sentence in exchange for his testimony."

Jenna inhaled sharply. "So it's true. He really was moving people, not equipment?"

"You really didn't know?"

Jenna choked on something that sounded like a cross between a hysterical laugh and a sob. "I told you. I had no idea. He cut me off from everyone I knew. I let him take me away from my sister. It didn't even cross my mind he wasn't just…in love with me enough to want me all to himself. Until he hit me, I had no idea what he was doing to me, let alone to anyone else. He didn't let me see the other side of his life. In fact, he controlled everything I saw and everyone I talked to. He…" Her hands covered her eyes. "I didn't know him at all. And he didn't care about me at all." She edged the barest inch away from Wyatt.

With a sharp, stinging clarity, he knew. She expected every man to treat her like Cutter had. Like her mother had. To not care about her. To see her as less than human.

Even Wyatt.

He shot a hard look at Rich. He couldn't let her believe she was worth nothing to him.

Nance caught his attention, leaning forward in his chair. "You mean to—"

"What exactly is the problem Chief Thompson mentioned, sir?" Wyatt wasn't going to let Nance grill Jenna until she fell apart. She'd had enough.

Nance glared at him. Wyatt had overstepped, the small-town cop running over the federal investigator.

He didn't care.

Chief Thompson intervened. "The men we took into custody at Christa's farm are talking. They work for Grant Meyer. He's purchased land north of town under an alias, looking to create a stop on a north-south pipeline, exactly like you suspected all along, Wyatt. One of his men spotted Jenna, who looks—"

"Exactly like her sister." Wyatt sat on the couch and stared at the painting of Anson's Ridge above the fireplace. "How does something like that happen? What kind of huge coincidence brought him to the same place Jenna ran?"

"No coincidence." For the first time, Nance looked compassionate, but he squelched it so fast Wyatt wasn't sure he'd seen correctly. "Ms. Clark, your real name is Genevieve Brady. Who helped you get a new identity? Who helped you move here?"

She gasped. "No. No. No." It was almost as though she couldn't think enough to say any more. "He would never point them to me."

"Anthony Reynolds didn't reveal your location."

"You know about Anthony?"

A slight smile tipped Agent Nance's lips, then vanished. "Anthony Reynolds has worked for us for years. We've fed him resources, new papers and identities, in return for information. He led us to a lot of bad people, including Logan Cutter. However, we had no idea he'd used those resources to make you disappear until one of our agents spotted you while we were here investigating the truck. We knew Amy Brady's twin sister had vanished, but we were working under the assumption that Cutter had killed you."

Jenna gasped, then dug her teeth into her lip. She was probably thinking how close their suspicions had almost been to the truth.

Wyatt wanted to ask Nance to step outside and have a conversation about tact.

"The thing is…" Nance scratched his cheek, then shifted his phone to his thigh. "Anthony Reynolds tucked you away here in Mountain Springs because he knew the area. He was hiding you from Logan Cutter, not from Grant Meyer, who'd been scouting here over a decade ago until he decided the area was too remote. He had Reynolds do the legwork when he was first checking out this area. Problem was, when he went underground, he had to rely on his past intel, so he went with what he'd already researched and started to look in this area again."

"And Anthony didn't warn me?"

"Anthony Reynolds is currently in protective custody in a secure location. Someone ratted him out to Meyer." There was another flash of compassion. "We need to get you into hiding as well. Fast. Word is out about you living here, and Meyer has offered his men a reward for your sister. He doesn't have a lot of men left, but every one of them is after Amy Brady. We're going to put you in a safe house." He turned to Wyatt. "You're going with her. We have a place—"

"Why?" Jenna rose and aimed a finger out the window. "You're all forgetting. My sister is dead. Grant Meyer killed her. Why would he put a price on the head of someone he already murdered? It doesn't make sense!"

But it did. Everything clicked into place, and Wyatt nearly rocked backward. He looked at Chief Thompson then at Agent Nance, who refused to meet his eye.

The dodge was all the confirmation Wyatt needed. He stood and reached for Jenna's hand, turning her to him, wishing for a way to cushion his next words, knowing there wasn't one. "Because, Jen…your sister is alive."

TWELVE

Your sister is alive.

Jenna stared at the highly polished dark hardwood between her feet, the smell of fresh paint and new everything about to upend her stomach. The corporate apartment they'd moved her to in Asheville was brand-new, sporting high-end furniture and the latest, greatest appliances.

She'd better not be here long. It had been hours since she'd arrived with Agent Nance. Night had passed and the sun had risen an hour or so ago.

Of course, locked up in this apartment, the time of day, the weather, the location... None of it mattered. The view she'd seen from the one time she'd peeked between the blinds had revealed nothing but the brick of the building next to this one. It was too much city, too much of a reminder of the life Genevieve Brady had left behind when she became Jenna Clark.

Too much.

Your sister is alive.

How? There hadn't been an answer beyond Wyatt's declaration. There hadn't been time. Wyatt had dropped his bombshell between them and before the fallout from the explosion could settle, her life whiplashed again. The female agent who had been in her shop the day before arrived, and someone introduced her as Agent Howell. She changed into Jenna's favorite outfit and gave Jenna her clothes and hat. Agent Nance had whisked her away to Asheville, leaving Wyatt with Agent Holmes and Chief Thompson to depart later as a diversion.

Jenna hadn't said a word since Wyatt's statement had shattered the rest of the illusions in her world. How had he known? She couldn't decide if she was angry, hurt... or just numb. She'd simply followed orders, too rocked to be more than a sheep herded by an entire army of shepherds.

Across the room, Agent Nance sat at a small table, a computer and several files open in front of him. He'd said little on the drive here, his longest speech the one he'd given her as they entered the apartment. "Here's your bedroom. Here's the kitchen. Oh, and stay away from doors and windows."

His silence filled her with a rushing fury. He had answers about her life. Answers she needed.

Shoving off the couch, Jenna stalked across the room and stood over the man who seemed to know more about her life than she did. "Where is my sister?"

Agent Nance shut the laptop and shuffled a few papers before he acknowledged her. "Your sister?"

"Wyatt said she's alive. How is she alive? Where is she? When can I see her?"

"Ms. Brady, I—"

"Clark. Ms. Clark."

"Okay. Ms. Clark, I never said your sister is alive." When Jenna moved to argue, he held up one finger, then shoved his chair away from the table and stood, towering over her. "And even if she was, WITSEC is deep. Even I wouldn't be able to tell you anything."

"So how did Wyatt know?"

"I can't answer for what Officer Stephens knows or doesn't know. That's on him. I can't even verify for you if what he said is true."

"She's my sister. Find someone who knows." If Amy was alive, Jenna wanted to see her, to make things right, to restore their family. She hadn't realized how desperately strong the desire was until Wyatt had spoken hope out loud. "Please."

Nothing in Agent Nance's expression changed. He simply stared down at her for a few seconds, then turned away. "I'm making breakfast. Would you like anything?" Without waiting for an answer, he walked away.

Jenna nearly followed him, then stopped. He wouldn't give her any answers. He was trained not to. His job was to rush her from place to place, to hide her from the bad guys. To keep her moving so fast no one could catch her.

Maybe not even Wyatt.

She hadn't even told him goodbye.

Hadn't Agent Nance said Wyatt was coming with her? Hadn't Wyatt promised he'd protect her?

Jenna trudged to the couch and sat, numb hopelessness replacing the fire that had flared for a moment. Maybe Wyatt's promise was only valid as long as he was in her presence. Maybe she'd imagined everything between them. Maybe she was asleep and when she awoke, the past three years would all be a dream.

No. She wouldn't even wish such a thing. If this was all a dream, then she would wake up as the Genevieve Brady who still lived under Logan Cutter's roof with no control over her own life and no knowledge of the Jesus who'd saved her.

With everything happening to tilt her world sideways, maybe God had abandoned her, too.

A shadow moved in front of her, and something heavy thunked on the overly modern glass coffee table.

Jenna lifted her head as Agent Nance backed away and resumed his seat at the small café table near the kitchen. The familiar warm scent of coffee lifted from a bright red mug resting in front of her.

Nance was watching, gauging her reaction. "I got a text a few minutes ago. Officer Stephens said to make sure you got coffee at the first chance."

Jenna blinked twice, then stared at the mug. He was thinking of her, telling her so in the only way he could communicate.

Why? It made no sense. Why reach out to her when he'd promised to stay with her, then let her go?

Tears pushed at the backs of her eyes. She stood abruptly, stalked to the bathroom next to the small master bedroom and leaned against the door. She hung her head, letting the tears slide silently down her cheeks. She couldn't do this any longer. This running and uncertainty was worse than when she'd left El Paso. There, she'd had nothing to lose. Here, she had everything to lose.

She had Wyatt to lose. The way he'd been acting since they were rescued out of the fire, she'd probably already lost him.

Her heart jolted. The idea of Wyatt being gone hurt worse than the loss of her identity, than the loss of her shop.

When had that happened?

Three years of shoving him away, of sniping at him every time he came around, of bristling at his presence... Those emotions and habits didn't simply go away in a few days' time. The two of them had been at odds practically since the first time she'd laid eyes on him, when he'd come by the shop while Erin was helping her paint. He'd walked in to her space, confident and totally Wyatt, looking around like he owned the place. Those broad shoulders of his had filled out his uniform like it was cut for him. His half smile had squeezed at his eyes just so. Something about him almost made the light in the room different.

That day, her bruised heart had jumped at the first sight of him. She *hadn't* been fighting him ever since.

She'd been fighting herself.

Her aversion to him had been nothing other than fear. Fear of rejection. Fear of once again being treated like someone's possession.

Fear of what he could become in her life forced her to push him away every chance she got.

Because everything in her, from the very first moment, had been drawn to him. Never anyone else. Only Wyatt.

And he'd betrayed her. Had left her behind after he'd promised to stay, exactly like all of her mother's boyfriends. Had known her sister was alive and hadn't found a way to hold her close. He was as bad as every other man she'd ever known.

Yet he'd put himself in danger for her. Had disobeyed his chief to stay with her. Had held her each time another piece of her world crumbled. He'd been all about her and her alone since the moment he rescued her in the alley behind her store.

So which Wyatt was he?

Pressing her spine into the door frame, she straightened, then went to the sink and splashed her face with cold water. She couldn't do this right now. Wyatt wasn't here, so there was no need to fret over him. She had bigger things to do. A bigger person to be. Somehow, she had to wrest away the controls to her life.

Jenna jerked open the door and marched across the bedroom.

A figure appeared in the doorway, shadowed by the light from farther up the hallway into the darkened bedroom. Broad shoulders, confident stance...

Her heart stuttered.

Wyatt. He was here. He'd come back for her.

He should have stayed away.

Wyatt had steeled himself, prepared to keep his emotions firmly in check until this was all over. But the entire night, playing the game, pretending Agent Howell was Jenna in order to throw off anyone who might be watching... Driving her to a local airstrip to put her on a plane with two other agents in a ruse that would hopefully make Grant Meyer think they'd flown his quarry out of town...

The whole time, all he'd wanted was to be by Jenna's side. He'd done his job, had played his part, but every unoccupied inch of his mind had strained to return to her. To know she was okay. To make sure her emotions hadn't completely shattered under the weight of all she'd been through and learned as her life literally burned around her.

Standing in front of her, all of his preparation fell away. In the dim light leaking in from the hallway, it was obvious she'd been crying. Her eyes were bloodshot. Her nose was red.

She stood rooted in the center of the room, staring at him with something between surprise and anger.

He'd never wanted to reach out to a woman so much in his life. He wanted to wrap his arms around her and tell her he was sorry. She needed him, and he'd left her.

Jenna inched closer, hard eyes pinned on his. "How could you?" Her voice came out low and hard, a tone he'd never heard from her before, even in the past, when she'd been berating him.

Wyatt's head tilted to one side. "How could I what?" Leave her? Come back? What?

"You knew about my sister. You knew Amy was alive. How could you not—"

"I had no idea." She thought he'd been lying to her, withholding the most important information in her life. It wasn't true. He'd merely been the one to figure out what was being said between the words, to break the news that this was bigger than any of them had dreamed. "Jenna. That's not…" Wyatt dragged his hand across the top of his head, trying to coax out the words when he all he wanted was to touch her. "The way Agent

Nance was talking, the things he was saying… There was only one way Grant Meyer coming after you made sense, and that was if your sister is still alive. All of this only makes sense if she's in WITSEC and somehow Meyer found out." He stepped into the room, standing close enough to hear Jenna breathe. His heart physically ached for her and all she'd had to endure as the hits kept slapping her. "If I had known, believe me, I'd have told you. I wouldn't have let you live with your grief any longer than you had to."

The truth found its mark. Jenna crumbled, seeming to fall apart before his eyes. Grief, confusion, fear, pain, uncertainty… The emotions played out across her expression. She choked on a sob, then covered her face with her hands.

Wyatt's heart officially tore in two. Forget it. Forget everything. He was one man. Agent Nance could take care of protection detail. Jenna needed someone who cared solely about her heart.

Wyatt grabbed her hands, lowered them between them, then slipped his hands to her elbows. He wrapped his arms around her, leaving her with nothing to do but bury her face in his chest, her arms curled between them. Lately, this seemed to be the place she found herself most of the time.

He was perfectly fine with that.

Much like the night in her apartment, he couldn't calculate how long he held her as she poured out her pain. When she pulled in a shuddering breath and tried to put distance between them, Wyatt tightened his arms around her and held her close. She was protected in the here and now. Nothing would get through him to her. If she backed away, he couldn't guarantee how long safety would last. The past few hours had proven to him with dead certainty he needed to know she was safe if he was going to function enough to see this through to the end.

Jenna pressed her forehead against his chest. "Anthony knew about Grant and Logan all along." Her voice was muffled in his shirt, her breath warm through the fabric.

It wasn't the direction he'd expected her to go, but he'd follow. "He was helping to stop them."

"But he didn't warn me or Amy."

"Maybe he figured it all out after you left. It could be what happened to you tipped him off." It made sense. From what she'd told him, he was protective of the sisters, and he knew what Cutter had done to her. Anthony Reynolds would view taking down Logan Cutter and Grant Meyer as the perfect opportunity to make sure someone he cared for stayed safe forever. He'd put his own reputation and life on the line for them.

Wyatt could understand the feeling.

"And Amy's alive."

There it was. The real issue. He rested his chin on her head. "You know I have no confirmation other than a hunch. I tried to talk to Agent Howell, but she wouldn't say anything."

"Neither would Nance." She tugged against him and he let her back up, though he kept his hands at her hips, not letting her get too far. He wasn't ready to break whatever this connection was, to walk out of this room and into a world intent on tearing her apart.

Lifting the flower charm from where it rested at her

neck, she held it on one finger. "Amy wore this all of the time. Never took it off. Anthony gave it to her one Christmas. It's an…" She smiled a watery smile. "It's an amaryllis."

"And now you wear it."

"Thing is, the only way she'd ever take it off is if she was…" Jenna sniffed. "She'd never take it off."

Wyatt rested his finger on the charm, her finger warm against his, then he lifted his eyes and let them sweep hers.

She was looking up at him, her gaze intense but more at peace than it had been a few minutes before. The tears had been good for her. Her eyes still held a watery sheen that made them a brighter green than usual, almost otherworldly, a color he couldn't tear himself away from. A strand of hair caught in her eyelash, making her blink.

Tugging his hand from hers, he brushed the strand aside, then lifted his hand and ran it along her hairline, his fingers brushing the scar he'd noticed at Christa's. She'd cringed then when he touched it. "Where did the scar come from?"

"Logan." She said the name flatly, in a matter-of-fact tone, the same way someone would say they'd burned a finger on a stove or bruised their thumb with a hammer.

As though it was normal, no big deal.

No. His whole body ached for her pain, for what she'd endured physically and emotionally at the hands of a man who'd treated her like his property in such a subtle way she hadn't even realized what was happening until it was too late.

Wyatt wanted to make her pain go away forever. All

of it. From her mother's neglect to her sister's death to Logan Cutter's cruelty. "I'm sorry." His whisper was so low she probably didn't hear it, but he still had to say it. Somehow, the guilt was his for not being there to protect her even before he'd ever met her. "You are worth so much more than you think you are." What was the verse his mom had taught him? "So much more than the sparrows God takes care of." *Sparrows*. She was like them. Strong enough to fly, yet so, so delicate.

So in need of protection.

Without caring about anything outside of the space between them, he drew her closer with the hand still on her hip and brushed a kiss across the scar, her skin warm beneath his lips.

Her hands slipped from his chest to his cheeks, her palms against his jaw, her fingers splayed at his cheeks. She turned his head toward her until they were forehead to forehead, nose to nose, so close her breath brushed his lips as she whispered in a way that he felt more than heard. "You're not him." There was a wonder, a knowing, as though she'd discovered something she hadn't been searching for.

Wyatt crumbled. He closed the small space between them, his lips brushing hers once, resting for a moment on the soft skin at the corner of her mouth before he slipped back and found her again, offering a promise he would never turn away from as she drew him closer and met him, accepting the safety he offered.

Nothing would every hurt Jenna Clark again. Ever. Not as long as Wyatt had breath in him.

THIRTEEN

Jenna sank into Wyatt, into his kiss. Everything else drifted away. Here and now, she was safe. Nothing could touch her.

Wyatt Stephens was the opposite of almost every man she'd ever known. He cared about her. Put her first. Shielded her. Took an interest in her. Made her feel as though she was important, as though there was nothing else in his life outside her. So unlike Logan. So unlike her mother's many, many conquests.

You're not him. He wasn't. Wyatt was so much more. He was solid ground. An anchor. The last stable thing she had left.

She hadn't known it could be like this. Had never realized she could feel utterly safe with a man, one who had promised to protect her, had proven he would keep his promise countless times.

Had put his life on the line for her over and over again.

His life. For hers. The last stable thing she had left.

Jenna gasped, her fingers slipping from Wyatt's cheeks. She couldn't let him stand in the line of fire for her again. She wouldn't. If something happened to him because of her…

Wyatt's hands eased away from her as though he was reluctant to let go. His gaze was hooded, a mix of confusion and emotion as though he'd been completely lost in her and she'd slapped him into reality.

Jenna backed one more step away from him. For a brief moment, she'd lost herself. She'd let herself believe things with Wyatt could be different. And maybe they could be.

Maybe.

If they both survived.

Her head swung from side to side, an involuntary negative, a *no* that tore at her heart as his expression shifted from desire to questions. "Jenna…"

"I can't do this."

His jaw tightened. "You can't do what?" The words ground out between clenched teeth, but it wasn't anger. It was hurt. Rejection.

Jenna knew the emotion all too well, but she couldn't apologize. Couldn't reach over and make it all better. If she did, there'd be no way to save him, no way to make sure he lived until this was all over and she could tell him the truth… The truth that he was now holding her very fragile heart in his very strong hands.

"You can't do what, Jenna? Care about me? Trust me? Believe I'm not like everybody else?"

The intensity of his questions nearly broke her. Sure, she'd told him she knew he was different, but she couldn't say it again, couldn't reassure him how much she knew it with everything in her, not if she wanted to protect him. After this was over and she was safe, she would find him again, she'd tell him.

If he'd still have her.

"You have to leave."

"I have to…what?" He looked incredulous, and the slight arrogance that had always coated their dealings with one another slipped into his expression. The old Wyatt. The one she'd done battle with so many times before.

The one who had been gathering little pieces of her heart since the first moment she'd laid eyes on him.

This was the precise reason he couldn't stay. Too many times he'd been in danger because of her. Her eyes roamed his face, landing on the scrapes that highlighted his cheekbone. He'd been attacked in the alley the very first night, nearly killed because of her. He'd been beside her in Christa's studio and in the fire, both of their lives in equal danger. If he stayed, if he continued with this insane drive to put himself between her and death, eventually he'd catch what someone was aiming at her.

She might physically survive such an encounter, but it would kill her all the same.

"You have to go to Mountain Springs." Jenna turned away from him as his eyes widened slightly. "You have to…go."

"Uh-huh." The utterance slipped out in a way that sounded as though he hadn't meant for it to. "Okay. No."

"Wyatt. Please." The desperation in her voice would give her away if he caught it.

"The answer's no." Every trace of emotion had been stripped from his voice. His words were plain, matter-of-fact and totally commanding. "I don't know what game you're playing, but you should know games are the last thing I'll stand for."

Her mouth opened, closed. She wavered and nearly turned, but her resolve kicked in and she hardened her expression. He couldn't see how much this was hurting her. He simply had to leave.

"I have no idea what you think is happening here, either with Meyer or between us, but games are dangerous. You of all people should know they are. But you understand this—as long as you're in danger, I'm not leaving. Ever. You should have figured that out about me by now, Jenna, but maybe..." He exhaled loudly and as he walked away, his footsteps fell softly on the hardwood, his voice coming from farther away, near the door this time. "Maybe neither of us knows the other as well as I thought."

The door whispered almost silently and clicked softly shut behind him.

Jenna sank to the edge of the bed and stared at the door, fighting the urge of her muscles to chase him, wishing he'd throw the door open and refuse to let her push him away.

He didn't come back, and she didn't follow him. It was for the best, the only way. If she survived this, if she came out on the other side still breathing, then... Then she could tell him he'd managed to do the impossible.

To put together the pieces of her shattered heart.

It didn't matter, though. Whatever it was he'd been saying about value and the sparrow verse she'd heard so many times...none of it mattered. Because in the end, she knew what she was worth, knew the only thing she was good for was being left behind.

Wyatt wanted to put his fist through the wall. Seriously. Straight through the Sheetrock. And if he hit a stud in the process, so much the better. The pain in his hand would surely eclipse the pain in his chest.

Doubtful.

The pain in his chest might kill him.

Wyatt turned and stared at the door he'd closed behind him. He'd left his heart on the other side. Had ripped it out of his chest, handed it to Jenna Clark, and she'd ground her heel into it.

Aiming to protect herself, to hold her heart out of reach. Exactly like Kari. She'd drawn him in. Had made him feel. Had dragged his head right out of sane, rational thought. He'd let her do it.

And it had cost him. Again.

Exactly. Like. Kari.

He'd known better than to get involved with a woman who was adept at deception. Who'd made it an art form in order to survive.

In order to survive. His shoulders stooped, the fight leaking out with his own unfairness. No. This time with Jenna was nothing like Kari.

Kari had lured him in. She'd baited the hook with a look and set it with a toss of her fiery red hair. They'd been at a backyard party, celebrating his buddy's marriage. Wyatt was nineteen, away from home, missing the anchor of family. There'd been some jealousy, too. O'Bryan was starting a life, would have someone to come home to, a place to lay his head other than a barracks room.

Someone to wait for him while he was deployed and to be there when he marched back in a year later.

If only Wyatt had been smart enough to recognize his own weakness. Kari had spotted his need for someone to care about him from across the yard and sashayed right in. She'd been the one to take the lead with their relationship, short as it had been, a whirlwind in the months leading to deployment. She'd been the one to float the idea of a wedding, of how romantic it would be to send him off as his wife and welcome him back to their very own home.

And he'd swallowed the hook. Infatuated, puffed up with the idea a beauty like her wanted to be his forever.

That beauty had been playing games with his life. Calculating his hazardous duty pay and hoping for the payoff of a fat insurance check if he returned in a flag-draped coffin.

His heart had iced over.

Until Jenna.

Wyatt fixed his gaze on the closed door, his ear straining to hear movement, to hear her come looking for him.

There was nothing but silence.

Jenna wasn't Kari. She'd never pursued him. In fact, from the first time he'd met her, she'd done anything but. She'd held him at arm's length, trying to hide the truth.

But not for the same reasons as Kari. Kari had been manipulative. Jenna had been fighting to survive.

He'd given her zero reason to trust him until a few days ago. His gut had skewed him sideways every time she was around, reacting to her in a way that sounded the alarm to steer clear. He'd thought it was because she was hiding.

Now, having held her in his arms... Having let her into his head and heart... Having kissed her...

It was so much more. He could still see her the first time he'd met her. He'd been about to go on duty, wanting to check on Erin, who'd made a fast friend of the stranger in town.

Wyatt didn't trust fast friends. Not after Kari.

He'd looked for his cousin at Jenna's shop, where they were painting the inside a funky teal green. Jenna and Erin had been laughing as they sang a nineties boy-band song banging through the speakers in the shop. Jenna had one streak of blue paint in her hair and another on her cheek.

Wyatt's jaw had nearly dropped. His heart had jumped, jolting in his chest like never before.

As quickly as it leaped, it had hardened against her.

He'd been afraid. Every single time he got around her, his heart pushed her away, because it knew. It knew the ice would crack for Jenna Clark.

His heart had failed, softening anyway. He knew because the ache of her turning away proved she'd destroyed every wall he'd ever built.

Wyatt reached for the door. He wasn't going to let her push him away, not this easily.

His fingers wrapped around the knob. He had no idea what he was going to say to her, but he had to—

"Stephens."

The call from the living room dropped his hand from the door, dragging his attention from the woman behind it.

Agent Nance stood at the end of the hall with Agent Howell right behind him. "If you're going to be a part of this, you need to be read in."

Wyatt glanced at the door then turned toward the two federal agents, torn between his duty and his desire. Exactly the dangerous place Rich had warned him not to be.

With a last glance at the door, he chose the duty that could save Jenna's life and strode up the short hallway past the other two bedrooms. With the blinds closed and the front door locked tight, the spacious apartment felt more like an underwater prison than a luxury Asheville rental.

Prisoner was probably exactly how Jenna felt right now.

Wyatt could feel the itch himself. As he took the seat Agent Howell indicated at the dining room table, he cast a glance toward the door. Time overseas in crowded markets, constantly alert for suicide bombers or shooters, had dampened his enthusiasm for crowds in a big way. He'd never liked them to begin with. Now, he barely enjoyed Mountain Springs when the tourist crowds picked up. While the only people who'd been in sight near the building when he arrived were a small group of gardeners a couple of buildings away, the space around him still felt overpopulated.

Being trapped in a brick-and-vinyl apartment building in the center of dozens of identical brick-and-vinyl apartment buildings fired an urge to roam. If he'd had any sort of leverage with this small federal team, he'd have insisted they go to Rich's place. The man had hundreds of acres on the side of one of the nearby mountains. Wyatt would have been a lot more comfortable defending a position from one of the many hunting cabins on Rich's property than he was here.

This apartment made no sense. Located on the second floor, the front door was their sole escape route, unless they wanted to drop Jenna off the balcony by the master bedroom, where she was currently hiding. Sure, like Jenna's apartment, there was only one way in…but there was also only one way out.

Nance turned to Wyatt as soon as everyone was settled around the table. "Ms. Clark trusts you more than anyone else, so we're bringing you into the investigation we've been conducting with your department for the past five months."

"Wait." Wyatt straightened and leaned closer to the table. "Five months? You've been partnered with my department for five months and I—"

"Need to know, Officer Stephens. We've been working closely with Chief Thompson, and he's been the only one to know about our presence since we announced we'd ended the investigation into the incident on Overton Road."

Wyatt sat back in the seat, staring at the blinds behind Agent Nance. He'd helped investigate the truck. He'd talked to the chief numerous times over the months, sharing suspicions, bouncing off ideas, keeping their eyes open, yet he'd been left completely out of the loop. Did Arch not trust him? Or was something more going on?

"Now isn't the time for your ego to get in the way." Nance flipped open his laptop and didn't spare another glance to Wyatt.

Anger flared, then cooled. The man was right. Rich's warning against emotions getting in the way didn't apply solely to his feelings for Jenna. It applied to all of them. He found the place that dropped him into sheer reason and focused on the agents before him. "What do I need to know?"

"So far, Grant Meyer has managed to evade arrest. A joint task force between the FBI, Homeland Security and local law enforcement in El Paso had him under surveillance, but he was tricky. Until Amy Brady passed us a hefty amount of information on his dealings, we had nothing solid. She agreed to dig deeper, to try to insinuate herself into his confidence so we could get enough information to put the nails in his coffin without any loopholes. Unfortunately, Meyer found out. Because we'd already managed to turn one man in his organization, we were able to intercept the hit. She was relocated."

"So she is alive."

"Yes."

"When can Jenna know?"

"When we know it's safe."

They couldn't ask him to keep this from Jenna. They had to know Wyatt wouldn't betray her. His leg bounced, urging him to go to her.

"Focus, Officer Stephens." Nance was all business.

And he was right. For now. "Let me guess. Your man on the inside was Logan Cutter. You offered him a deal, and he turned on Meyer." Figured. Cutter would get away with what he'd done to those women and to Jenna.

Wyatt balled his fists under the table. Except it hadn't quite worked out for him. Clearly, Meyer had found out and had the man killed a few months... "Wait." Timing clicked into place. "Meyer had Cutter killed. What are the odds Cutter let out the truth about Amy still being alive?"

"High." Agent Howell laid her hands flat on the table. "He got awfully close to her at one point and she had to be moved."

"So when someone spotted Jenna they assumed—"

"They assumed she was her sister," Nance said. "Amy Brady is the sole remaining link who can put Meyer's organization out of business for good. He knows she's a danger to him and will do anything to find her. We believe he's close by. He was spotted in Tennessee two days ago. There's only one reason he'd be heading east."

Agent Howell balled her fists. "And we will stop him."

Suddenly, everything made sense. The move to Asheville. The strange location of the apartment. The gardeners outside a secure location. Fire blew through Wyatt. He stood and looked at the two agents, fear for Jenna's life nearly melting his joints. "I know what you're doing."

Agent Nance rose. "Officer Stephens—"

"No. You want to use Jenna to draw out Meyer. That's the whole reason you're here. It's not to protect her. It's to get your man."

Reaching for a folder in the center of the table, Howell hesitated. "No one said such a thing." She glanced at Wyatt then at Agent Nance before she drew the folder closer, then reached back to tighten the band holding her straight brown hair in a ponytail.

Wyatt's adrenaline surged. From the small amount of time they'd spent together over the past few hours, he knew the FBI agent wasn't one to use a lot of words. He'd assumed there was little she could say, since he wasn't at their level of clearance.

But the move...the hesitation, the glance, the attempt to draw his attention to her looks by playing with her hair... She was hiding something. He'd seen Kari do the same thing many times when he'd asked her why she was running late or hadn't answered his calls for hours.

Freeze. Speak the lie. Touch her hair or her neck to distract him. Except with Kari, it was usually because she wanted to distract him when he grew suspicious of her motives.

With Agent Howell, it could simply be Wyatt's concern... Or it could be that she was playing a dangerous game with Jenna's life.

FOURTEEN

"I'm not letting you do this to her." Wyatt's voice came through the door, raised and angry.

Jenna stood from her perch on the side of the bed, where she'd been praying since he walked out. Praying for clarity. For safety. For an end to the nightmare.

Wyatt's words shattered the holy silence. She'd seen him irritated before, annoyed, even on the verge of losing his temper, but this? This bordered on rage. It shuddered inside her, an echo of Logan's fury the night he'd nearly killed her.

Jenna walked to the door and rested her hand on the knob. This time, the anger wasn't against her.

It was for her.

The peace she'd found in prayer, the certainty that she could trust Wyatt to have her back, washed over Jenna in a calm stillness, in a sense telling her she needed to follow wherever he led. *I'll do it, Lord, but please... Please don't let him get hurt.*

Footsteps thudded on the hardwood, coming closer.

"Stephens, you have no authority." Jenna backed

away from the door as Agent Nance's voice drifted up the hallway. "There's a team in place to protect—"

The words stopped abruptly as the door opened. Wyatt stood there, once again a silhouette, but this time, his stance was tense, his movements urgent. In the shadows, his eyes were hard as he reached out for her. "We have to get you out of here."

Jenna let him take her hand. "What's wrong?"

"I'm not…" He searched her face as though deciding what he wanted to say. "You're not safe here. We have to leave. Now."

"It's too late to get out of here." Agent Nance followed him into the doorway. "They already know. We've been tracking them since one of his men followed you here. It's only a matter of time before they arrive."

"Who's they? Who's coming?" Jenna's heart beat faster. She gripped Wyatt's hand tighter, her earlier peace shattered. "Wyatt?"

He never turned to her but kept his gaze fixed hard on Agent Nance in a staredown he seemed determined to win. "They're using you as bait. Meyer knows where you are. No one followed me here, so it must have been Agent Howell. Wherever the plane landed, they knew Meyer would be watching." Wyatt lifted his head and looked toward the living room. "You let them follow you here. Let them think they had the upper hand while you knew all along. And no one clued me in." He drew Jenna to him. "I'm supposed to be the one protecting her and no one clued me in." He ground out the last words as though they were gravel in his mouth.

Jenna pressed closer to Wyatt, fear tightening her

throat. Grant Meyer knew where she was. She was trapped. There was one way into the apartment and there was no way they could go waltzing out the front door without being seen.

Agent Nance held a hand up to Wyatt. "If you'd listened instead of walking away, you'd know there's a team outside, ready to intercept the moment they arrive."

"The grounds crew two buildings over? You really think such a diversion will work?"

"Yes. Ms. Clark is perfectly safe. We're all perfectly safe staying right in this apartment where we are. If Meyer is with them, this will all be over as soon as they choose to make a move."

"And if he's not?" Wyatt's voice was ice-cold, sending a shiver along Jenna's skin.

"If he's not, we look at a more permanent solution for keeping him from getting to Ms. Clark."

Enough. They were talking about her as though she wasn't right in front of them, as though her life no longer belonged to her and she no longer had the freedom to make her own decisions. "Wait. Stop." Three pairs of eyes turned toward her. "You think Grant Meyer is here? Nearby?"

"Yes." Agent Howell spoke from behind Nance. "We lost him in Tennessee but we believe he was headed here to confront you—well, your sister—personally."

"So if I let him get close, you can catch him? This will all be over? And Amy will be safe? She can come out of hiding?"

Agent Nance nodded, but Agent Howell's gaze kicked to the left, avoiding Jenna's eye.

The look crawled across Jenna's skin. Something was wrong. She let go of Wyatt's hand and stepped in front of him. "What are you not telling me?"

"Nothing." Agent Nance held her gaze, and this time she didn't look away.

"Where is my sister?" Jenna forced all of her fear, her grief, her frustration into the question. The words came out heavy and threatening, a voice she'd never heard from her own mouth before.

Even Wyatt stiffened behind her before he found her hand and twined his fingers with hers, urging her to keep asking.

Agent Howell pressed her lips into a tight line and had a silent conversation with Agent Nance before she spoke. "We don't know."

"What do you mean you don't know?" Wyatt took the lead now, moving to stand beside her, a united front. "You told me not five minutes ago you'd moved her for her own safety."

Nance exhaled loudly and motioned to the hallway toward the front of the apartment, urging them to move into the living room before he started to walk that way. "Yesterday, she vanished."

"You lost my sister?" Jenna let go of Wyatt's hand, squeezed past Agent Howell and followed Agent Nance into the living room. "How do you lose track of a person? You weren't watching her?"

"Your sister was living much the same way you were, under an assumed identity in a different state until Grant Meyer somehow located her. She was moved into protective custody briefly, given a new identity and moved again. Yesterday, she vanished."

Jenna wavered and collided with Wyatt, who laid his hands on her shoulders, supporting her. "Do you think—"

"No." Nance shook his head and crossed his arms over his chest. "If Meyer had her, he wouldn't be targeting you. Her home was processed. She deliberately packed a bag and left. There have been no hits on her credit cards or her identity since."

"Why would she leave?"

"We don't—" A rapid succession of pops from outside made Agent Nance whirl toward the window above the table.

Agent Howell turned to Wyatt, who'd pulled Jenna against him. "Get her into the bathroom. Into the tub. Lock the door and keep her out of sight until one of us comes for you."

Jenna's throat went dry. Her heart pounded. They were here. They really had come for her.

Wyatt's hands dropped from her shoulders, and he reached around her, tugging her with him. "Let's go." He dragged her up the hallway as the noises from outside stopped. "Move, Jen—"

The door exploded inward and bounced off the wall.

Wyatt grabbed Jenna, shoved her into the first bedroom on the left, pushed her into the walk-in closet and threw himself in front of her, dropping to one knee and drawing his pistol as shots roared in the apartment.

Stillness.

Silence.

Low voices and footsteps.

They'd kill Wyatt. Whoever was in the apartment would shoot him before he could fire a single round.

She couldn't let them. He couldn't die protecting her. She'd never be able to live with herself if she was responsible for the death of the man she loved.

Because she did. She'd never have imagined she could, never imagined her heart was even capable of that kind of trust, but she did. And because she loved him, she had to save him. He'd thrown himself between her and death more than once.

Wyatt had been right earlier. She had value…to the men outside the door.

It was her turn to make the sacrifice.

Wyatt kept himself between Jenna and the closet door as cautious footsteps rang up the hallway, loud on the hardwood. The eerie quiet following the flurry of gunfire and the faint smell of gunpowder told the tale…

Howell and Nance were either incapacitated or dead.

Whoever had killed them knew Wyatt was here. They wouldn't go easy on him, especially once they realized he was the last thing standing between them and their target. He wasn't sure how many there were in the apartment, but he'd take every single one of them down before he'd let them take Jenna.

Or he'd die trying.

The footsteps hesitated in the hallway outside the bedroom and Wyatt leveled his pistol at the closed closet door. More footsteps. Two sets, heavy and methodical, as though they were clearing the room, which meant they were likely highly trained.

Trained or not, it didn't matter. There were more of them than him, and he'd have to be ready if he wanted to get them both out of this alive.

Everything he'd ever trained for came down to this moment. Every military exercise. Every moment of police training. He was laser focused on the sounds outside the door, on protecting the woman he loved.

The woman he'd loved for as long as he could remember.

Every muscle in his body tensed, ready to face off in this final battle.

The footsteps, slow and methodical, sounded in the bedroom.

Wyatt slipped his finger to the trigger, heart pounding, sweat coating his forehead.

Behind him, Jenna shifted, then rose.

Panic raced through Wyatt. What was she doing? He couldn't block her if she was standing. He couldn't lower his weapon and drag her to safety without dropping his guard and possibly signing both of their death warrants. Had she lost her—

"I'm worth more to you alive than dead." Jenna's voice was too loud. It rang out clear and strong, nearly echoing off the empty closet walls.

The footsteps stopped.

"What are you doing?" Wyatt asked.

She didn't acknowledge him, but simply raised her voice again. "I'm alone and I'll come out. No fighting on my end. No shooting on yours. I'll go with you.

You get the full price for…" Her words stuttered, wavered. "For me."

"Jenna, no." His voice rasped, his heart thudding painfully in his chest. He wanted to turn to her, cover her mouth, stop her. But he couldn't take his attention from the door and the threat on the other side. Instead, he reached around with his free hand, his fingers wrapping around her ankle. "What are you doing?"

She eased around to stand beside him and whispered, "Saving your life." Laying a hand on his shoulder, she raised her voice again. "No one else dies. If they do, I fight. I fight you all the way. And you lose half of your money."

She was killing him. Literally killing both of them. Even if the men outside agreed to her terms initially, she'd be in their hands and they'd surely return to finish him off. Men like Grant Meyer didn't leave loose ends.

"Somebody heard those gunshots. There are probably police on their way now." Jenna raised her voice. "I'll fight all the way out of here and slow you down, and you know Meyer would rather have me alive after he was fooled the last time."

The silence was long, causing Wyatt's muscles to tense. His mind spun through plans. He could shove aside Jenna, burst through the door with guns blazing.

Except he didn't really know how many were out there, how many reinforcements they had, what weapons they carried. If he died trying to be a hero, there would be no one to protect Jenna.

He had no control. Zero. There was nothing he could do to make this work. Nothing. He couldn't save Jenna.

He was helpless, exactly like the day when he'd frozen outside the Pritchett house and two people had died.

Harsh whispers rose outside, a quick exchange that sounded like an argument.

"Come out slowly, hands up." A muffled voice came through the door. "You've got ten seconds."

Before Wyatt could lower his weapon and rise from his knee, Jenna slipped from his grasp, edged open the door and went out in a flurry of motion.

Out. Between him and the men trying to take her. No clear line of fire. No clear way to save her except to show himself.

They weren't going to get her out of this apartment. Not if he could stop them.

Sliding to the side of the door, Wyatt peered out through a crack, then eased out of the closet into an empty room. They were moving fast. Too fast.

Staying on the balls of his feet to keep his footfalls silent on the hardwood, Wyatt edged to the door, the pounding in his ears overtaking nearly every sound from the front of the apartment.

Pistol at the ready, he peeked around the threshold and into the living room. Two men, masked. The lead man had Jenna in front of him, one arm around her and the other hand holding a pistol against her side. He was focused on the door.

The other man was slightly to the right, holding a shotgun, covering the living room where the FBI agents were likely dead or injured.

He couldn't get a shot off without risking Jenna. They were packed too tightly together.

But that didn't mean he couldn't follow.

He slipped into the hallway as a soft sound from the living room made the man holding the rifle spin around, his weapon raised…his eyes on Wyatt.

There was something about those eyes…

There was a shout. A blow to Wyatt's torso, the crack of gunfire. Wyatt dropped, his ribs burning, his breath gone…

And Jenna was screaming.

FIFTEEN

"Wyatt!" His name tore from her throat, raw and painful. She'd surrendered herself. She'd done what they asked, what she'd promised.

They'd killed Wyatt anyway. He'd dropped in the doorway to the bedroom, his hands gripping his midsection, gun on the floor at his side, unmoving.

No.

Jenna screamed again and jerked toward him, nearly freeing herself, but hands dug into the back of her hair, dragging her backward until an arm wrapped around her waist and lifted her off the ground.

She fought, kicking and clawing, throwing her head back, trying to make contact with something, anything. She had to get free. She had to get to Wyatt. She had to do something, to—

The man holding her lowered her feet as her heel grazed his shin. He grabbed her chin and jerked her head backward so hard her neck cracked, firing spots through her vision. His fingers dug into her cheek and jaw and he jerked her head tight against his, twisting her head painfully to the side. "I won't hesitate to break your neck right here. Half of the money my boss wants for you is better than me sitting in prison for the rest of my life with nothing because you fought me all the way out of here."

Jenna froze, a whimper escaping her dry throat, and she hated herself for it. He meant it. He would kill her.

She wasn't sure it mattered anymore.

The second man, the one who'd shot Wyatt, spoke. "Lay off, man. You don't need to hurt her. You got what you wanted."

"Yeah, well… I did. And Meyer's getting her alive, so it's better for me, but I won't go to prison for a lousy extra hundred grand." He jerked Jenna closer to him. "Don't think for one second I trust you, either. You shot that one cop, sure. Proved you're serious. But there's nothing to say you won't flip again and put a bullet in me if it suits your purpose." Finally, his grip loosened slightly and allowed Jenna a deep breath. "Now, you will walk down those stairs like you have some common sense and you will do exactly as we say or I will shoot you in the stomach. You'll die slowly enough to watch us put a bullet in every single police officer who responds. Every one. Their deaths will be your fault. Maybe you'll bleed out. Or maybe you'll live and know you killed them all." He gripped her chin harder, dragging out another pained whimper. "Understood?"

Tears stung her eyes from the pain both internal and external. They had her. There was nothing she could do but go with them.

With a meek nod, she surrendered and walked quietly down the stairs, the pistol still digging into her spine. She could run, but it wouldn't end there. They'd kill others to spite her. Someone else would die as her punishment.

As sirens drew closer, they dragged her along the small lawn at the rear of the building, along a small ditch and into the parking lot of an apartment behind the one where she'd been hiding. The first man climbed into the driver's seat of a large SUV while the man who'd shot Wyatt jerked open the back door and shoved her to the floor, then climbed in behind her and planted a foot between her shoulder blades to keep her from rising.

They'd driven maybe five minutes, through several turns that further weakened her already rocking stomach, when the SUV stopped abruptly and the driver leaned around to look down at her. "Something to make sure we get you to your destination without any incidents."

A sharp, stabbing pain pinched her neck, and a burning sensation spread beneath her skin and into her head. "What was…" She blinked, her vision blurring, the words refusing to form.

"Enjoy your ride, Amy." He spit out her sister's name as though it was bitter. The sound came from far away, an echo at the end of a tunnel.

Her sister's name. He'd called her Amy. In the running and the fear and the death, she'd forgotten this wasn't about her. Grant Meyer had a price out on Amy's head, not hers. She wasn't the target.

Her sister was.

Maybe, if she fully surrendered and let Meyer destroy her, then he'd think he'd finally killed her sister. Maybe Amy could finally be free. The thought clung, stuck, swirled in her head until the pressure on her back released and the world faded to black.

* * *

Wyatt groaned and tried to roll onto his side, but a wave of nausea overcame him. He fought to surface from the faraway, drifting place his mind tried to take him. He had to sit up, assess the damage.

He'd been shot. They'd taken Jenna.

With a groan that broke through the grogginess, he moved his hands away from his side and lifted them, staring, his vision clearing.

Something was wrong. They felt dry. They were… dry. And clean.

No blood.

No blood?

With another groan, he pushed himself to rest against the wall and sat up, staring at the place the bullet had struck. He'd been shot. He'd heard the shot, felt the bullet hit, but… Nothing?

Voices and shouts penetrated the fog, but he lifted his shirt instead of turning to them. A huge angry reddish-purple bruise was forming on his lower rib cage. Probably a broken rib. But…the bullet?

He shook his head. Tried to breathe. Tried to bring focus into the world as the pain ebbed slightly and his senses came back online. The smell of gunpowder. The wail of sirens drawing closer.

Lots of sirens.

A shadow fell over him. Wyatt scrambled for his gun, but a hand on his shoulder stopped him.

"Stephens. Be still. If they broke your rib, you don't want to puncture a lung." Agent Nance kneeled beside him, his brown hair mussed, his own face etched in white lines of pain.

"They got Jenna." Wyatt tried to stand. "I have to go after her."

"Not yet." Nance held him down. "Local law enforcement is close. Someone must have called 911. We need to identify ourselves, let them clear us so we don't get shot in the process of getting out of here. They'll have paramedics, too. Let them get a look at you, then you can run off and try to find her."

"Are they gone?" Maybe Jenna was still nearby. Maybe whoever had taken her had been confronted by the police already.

"They got away. Clean. And we have no idea where they took her. Our men outside..." He stopped and clenched his fists. "Howell and I are fine. Most of them didn't fare so well."

Wyatt settled against the wall, willing the ringing in his ears to stop. Men were dead. Good men, killed by ruthless thugs who now had Jenna, and he couldn't do anything until local law enforcement let them go.

They'd better hurry. He had to get to Jenna before Meyer exacted his revenge on her. But Nance was right. The sirens were right outside. Even if he made it to the door, he didn't have a badge on him. Just a gun. With shots fired, this could only end with him surrendering and having to sort everything out before he could leave. Better to let the Feds read the locals in quickly so they could move. "What happened?" Intel. He needed intel. "How many? How did they...? What were they shooting? They hit me, but..." His voice was gaining strength, but when he breathed he still felt stabbing pain in his right side.

"There were two. One subdued our men outside and one busted in and hit me and Howell."

"You were shot?" But how? Nothing made sense. It was like the world was a thousand miles away, even as the pain cleared.

"We're okay." Agent Nance reached across Wyatt and lifted something from the floor. "Beanbag rounds."

"What?" Wyatt grabbed his gun from the floor, slid it into its holster, then planted a hand on the agent's shoulder and pushed himself to stand, the pain lifting slightly as he stood upright and took the pressure off of his rib cage. Bracing one hand against the wall, he held out his other, and Nance dropped the small beanbag round into his palm. A nonlethal solution, the rounds could be loaded into a 12-gauge shotgun and fired. They typically didn't kill, but they could cause enough damage to stun a victim into inaction long enough for them to get Jenna out of the apartment. The pain in Wyatt's ribs left no doubt. "You said they took down some of your men outside, but not us. Why not kill us all?" He held out a hand and helped Nance stand, shooting pain from his side throughout his body. He couldn't have a broken rib. If he did, they'd have to tape him up in the parking lot, because he wasn't going to any hospital.

He was going after Jenna.

"No idea. Meyer's men have proven they're not above killing. Sometimes they almost act as if they glory in it. But this?" His expression shadowed. "This makes me wonder."

"Wonder what?"

A rustle from the end of the hall made them turn their heads, Wyatt with his hand on his pistol.

Howell appeared, one hand on her stomach and one sweeping her brown hair away from her forehead. "He thinks it's an inside job and I wouldn't hesitate to agree. This is the work of someone who's after the money but not willing to kill to get it. Not the typical operating procedure for the kind of guys Meyer attracts."

The pain alone was enough to make Wyatt sick. Nance's theory made his stomach dive lower. He focused on the beanbag round in his hand, the weight of it heavier with each passing second. "I recognize this. At least, I think I do." He closed his fingers around the round and looked at the two federal agents, who were watching him closely. "Mountain Springs is a small department, but we keep a handful of these on hand as a precaution. This brand. I'm not saying it's one of my guys, but…" But there was a slim possibility. "He leave any shell casings behind?"

"Haven't looked."

The sirens outside grew louder and car doors slammed.

Agent Nance turned toward the door and pulled out his badge, prepared to identify himself when the police entered.

Howell picked up an object near the door and tossed it to Wyatt, who flipped the shell over in his hands, his pulse accelerating. "Make this quick with the locals and get me to Mountain Springs." Wyatt tightened his grip on the shotgun shell he held, his last link to the person who'd stolen Jenna. "I can tell you exactly where she is."

SIXTEEN

"How much did you give her?" The words cut through the gray darkness, pounding into Jenna's brain even though they sounded far away. Her head throbbed with each heartbeat. She tried to ease her eyes open but the light was too bright. Too intense. It assaulted her senses, stinging her nose and dragging tears to her eyes. She moaned once, twice, tried to dig her fingernails into what felt like rough wood to keep the room from spinning.

Her senses came back slowly. The voices had lowered. Something smelled like dirt and an old, closed-up house. Damp. Musty. Where was she?

The last thing she remembered she was… She was… With Wyatt? No. Wyatt was… She inhaled sharply, the breath shuddering painfully in her throat. Gunshots. Wyatt. Dropping to the floor. Men stuffing her into a car, threatening her.

She came into full consciousness screaming, her voice hoarse and ragged.

"Are you kidding me?" A voice across the room cursed, then shouted, "Make it stop already."

Jenna swallowed her next scream and worked bleary

eyes open as a shadow kneeled in front of her and eased her to her feet, leaning her against what felt like a wall. It took so much effort to lift her head, to focus her eyes…

And when they did focus, she gasped, then melted in relief.

Officer Brian Early was looking at her, eyes dark with pity.

She was safe.

"She screams again, duct-tape her mouth shut. I can't handle it." The second voice from across the room was rough, harsh. "I get now why it was double to bring her to Meyer alive."

The hope swelling in her chest faded. Her head swung from side to side, a soft *no* escaping her lips. "Brian… Why?" He'd been the voice at the apartment, the one cautioning the other man. The one who'd shoved her into the back seat and planted a boot in her back.

It didn't compute. While she didn't know him well, Brian Early was a quiet, respectful officer. A man who, like Wyatt, did his job with professionalism and care, who loved his town and the people in it. "Why?"

His jaw tightened, his lips pressing tightly together as his eyes squeezed shut then opened again. "Meyer has my sister. He wired me. He could hear everything I said, knew everywhere I went…"

"No." Nina Early was a sophomore at Appalachian State, as outgoing as her brother was reserved. A small-town girl with a ready smile and a sense of humor that lit the room when she came by to paint at the shop or to grab a cup of coffee. If Grant Meyer had her…

What would he do with a girl like Nina?

She laid a hand on Brian's arm, torn between fear for her own safety and pity for the man who had been backed into a vicious dark corner. But her heart hardened as quickly as it had beat in sympathy. She lifted her chin, the room spinning less now. "You killed Wyatt. You—"

"I—" Footsteps on the porch silenced him, and he turned, dragging Jenna to her feet and easing her behind him.

She didn't want a killer's protection. Rage, grief and fear built inside her and she drew away, determined to plant a fist in his back, in his neck, wherever she could land a punch.

But the door opened, and a man appeared, flanked by two other men, who loomed over him. Dressed in jeans and a gray button-down shirt, Grant Meyer looked every inch the casual businessman he had once pretended to be.

Jenna froze. This was it. The end. There was no escaping now, not with the firepower he'd brought with him.

And not with the hate in his eyes when his gaze landed on Jenna.

"Hello, Amy." He smiled, self-satisfied and smug, as though he'd read her thoughts and knew she realized the hopelessness of her situation. "It's been a long three years."

Jenna said nothing. Maybe he'd kill her quickly, believe he had Amy and drop the search. All she had left in life was to save her sister. Unless…

She laid a hand flat between Brian Early's shoulder blades. "Please…"

His head dipped, his posture slumped. He glanced over his shoulder at her and shook his head. "I'm sorry." With a deep breath he turned to Grant Meyer, his spine straightening. "I did what you asked me to do. I want my sister."

"You don't call the shots."

Brian stood impossibly taller, blocking Jenna from Grant's view. "Where is she?"

The silence stretched, heavy and dark. Jenna tensed, squeezing her eyes shut. Meyer wasn't the kind of man who valued life. He'd kill Brian for bucking up to him if it suited his purposes. Her whole body ached, waiting for the gunshot that would silence Brian's argument forever.

"She's nearby. In the Scenic Heights Hotel. Room eighty-seven."

Brian moved for the door and Jenna lifted her head as his shadow fell away, leaving her vulnerable and unprotected as she faced the man who'd destroyed her sister's life and, by extension, her own.

He was watching Brian. "You can go in a minute. Let's make sure you brought me what I wanted first." Brian stopped as Grant aimed a finger at the wall beside the door. "Wait there."

And then, he turned his attention to Jenna, surveying her, studying her.

Jenna shivered and tried to shrink from his leering assessment, but her muscles froze, fear rocking her from the inside out as he closed the small space between them. He grabbed her chin, lifted it forcefully and turned her head from one side to the other, his fingers rough on already bruised skin. His smug look slipped. He reached up with his other hand, lifted her hair from her neck, and fingered the ends, his eyes narrowing.

His touch slithered through her. Jenna was going to be sick. Right now. It would be her last act before she died.

Grant Meyer's dark eyes hardened, and his nostrils flared slightly before hot, red rage coated his expression. He shoved Jenna away from him by her chin.

Her neck muscles screaming, she hit the floor hard, a cloud of dust mingling with pain to choke her.

Meyer whipped a pistol from his side holster and leveled it at Brian Early. "You brought me the wrong girl." His voice was low, so much more frightening than a shout.

Deadly.

The other man, Brian's apparent partner, rose from a scarred wooden table in the corner of the room. He stalked toward Jenna, his expression a mix of anger and fear. "He told me this was her."

"No." Brian stepped one foot away from the pistol pointed straight at his forehead. His voice remained strong. "This is Jenna Clark. This is the one your men told me I had to bring to you in order to get my—"

"No." Moving closer, Meyer held the pistol tight against Brian's forehead, pressing against skin, the point of contact from the barrel rapidly reddening.

Jenna tried to scramble backward, but an iron grip lifted her from the floor and held her forearms tight as she watched the two men locked in a death stare. She wanted to shut her eyes, to turn away, but fear left her paralyzed.

Grant Meyer knew she wasn't Amy. He would kill her the same way he'd killed so many before her, and then he'd continue his hunt for Amy until she was dead, too.

Her sacrifices, her pain, Wyatt's death... Everything had been for nothing. *Jesus, I tried. I tried. I tried.* It was a mantra, over and over, and it wouldn't stop.

Meyer pulled a deep breath in and lowered his weapon, tapping it against his thigh. "Amy Brady is a blonde. A natural blonde." He smiled a wicked smile and shook his head, turning to look at Jenna. He walked over, ran a hand along Jenna's cheek and lifted her hair again.

She jerked away, his touch shuddering through her like spiders.

"Her twin sister? Genevieve? A natural redhead." He ran his fingers through her hair again, then turned slightly to look at Brian. "One of the few I've ever met. It's actually striking."

"Maybe she... Maybe she dyed it. Hiding." Brian straightened, emboldened by his own words. "Look, I did what you asked. All I want is my—"

"I know women, Early. They're my business. They've made me a lot of money over the years. I've got clients around the world. Some couldn't care less what they get. They buy in bulk. Others? They're very...particular. And they don't like getting something fake. This girl here is a natural redhead. I know. I know well. Girls like her put a lot more in my pocket."

Jenna wanted to turn inside herself and vanish. The things he was saying, the way he talked… How many women had he treated like property, used to line his pockets, dismissed as inventory? A sob shuddered through her, pain digging into her stomach. She nearly doubled over, her knees weakening. She would have hit the floor if the hands holding her biceps hadn't tightened.

Brian's gaze bounced to Jenna then to Meyer, a look of fear swiftly covered over with defiance. "I did what you asked. Your men made a mistake. It's not my fault they got the wrong woman. I was only told to bring Jenna to—"

"A mistake?" Meyer ghosted a smile. "I've got four of my best men sitting in an FBI holding cell right now because of your *mistake*. I've lost my stop in Mountain Springs, which means I have to cut my losses on property I've already bought and drop more money into a new location. I've come out of hiding to be here, to confront Amy Brady face-to-face for what she did to ruin me." The gun tapped faster against the side of his thigh. "The Feds know it. They know I'm close. Your *mistake* could have cost me everything." He turned toward Jenna, eyes narrowed scanning her from her head to her feet, then back again.

Then he smiled. Sick, twisted…as though he owned her.

In one motion, he lifted his arm and pulled the trigger. The shot echoed in the room, a loud crack that rendered Jenna temporarily blind and deaf as she flinched.

Brian dropped.

Jenna screamed and jumped backward, nearly top-pling the man who held her. She turned her head to the side, slamming her eyes shut, wishing she could erase what she'd seen, praying she'd live long enough to forget.

"Get the car around to the front door." Meyer's foot-steps came closer on the old hardwood, his shoes beat-ing a death march. Laying a hand on each of Jenna's cheeks, he turned her toward him as the man behind her let go.

When she opened her eyes, Grant Meyer was staring at her. "The bullet he took was almost yours, but then I thought what a shame it would be to waste a beauty like you when you're worth so much more to me alive."

Cold dread washed over Jenna, hardening her mus-cles into iron. No. No. *No.* He wasn't going to kill her but… No.

She would walk out of here alive, but there were fates worse than death. So. Much. Worse.

Wyatt winced at the gunshot and pressed his back tighter against the oak tree in the woods along the edge of Brian Early's family hunting property, his grip on his pistol tightening. The old original log house sat in the center of a small clearing.

Jenna was inside. His aching side mocked him, the ibuprofen he'd taken from the paramedics doing little to touch the pain. *Please, Lord. Please don't let the shot have been for her.* Not when he was this close. Not when he could save her.

The radio in his ear whispered, "Eyes on Jenna. She's

standing." From his vantage point in the woods at the front of the cabin, Chief Thompson must have a better view than Wyatt.

Wyatt exhaled slowly, his heart racing. Jenna was safe for the moment. He peered around the tree again, careful to stay concealed, fighting dark memories.

Memories of the Iraqi desert.

Of the Afghan mountains.

Of a house not so different from this one, in the humid heat of a North Carolina summer, and two gunshots that rang out while he watched, wounded and helpless.

Here he was again. Watching. Wounded. In Asheville, he'd rushed the paramedics along, refusing to go to the hospital. They'd wrapped his ribs the best they could in the field and he'd raced to Mountain Springs to the station, where plans were already underway to rescue Jenna.

The shell from the beanbag round had told Wyatt all he needed to know. In permanent marker, familiar handwriting scrawled...

Early.

No one had seen or heard from Early since late the afternoon before, when he went off shift. His cell phone was off. Calls to his sister—his emergency contact—went unanswered. Everything made sense now... The way Meyer had known they were at Christa's. The beanbag rounds in the rifle. Somehow, Meyer had gotten to the other officer, and he was cooperating under duress, which meant they had two hostages, possibly three, since his sister seemed to have disappeared as well.

Brian Early wouldn't fire live rounds at law enforcement, ever... But he could make Meyer's men think he was by loading beanbag shells in a standard 12-gauge.

He'd left a message behind on those shells. The Early family had two properties, Brian's house in town and a small, rarely used hunting cabin a few miles into the mountains. Two teams were readying to locate Jenna, one team for each location. With permission granted to pull surveillance and nothing more, they'd moved out. Wyatt joined the small group making their way through the woods to set up a fragile perimeter around the Early cabin, certain the isolated location was the one Meyer would choose.

A hostage rescue team was en route from the FBI and a smaller unit was headed in from the state, waiting for surveillance to tell them which location was the right one.

The right one was the cabin.

Now, they waited. But the gunshot had nearly driven Wyatt to violate orders and rush in for the rescue. Someone was surely dead, and the next bullet might have Jenna's name on it.

Another radio transmission. "Movement."

Wyatt leaned around the tree again. A man jogged down the stairs and headed for the dark blue SUV sitting near the front corner of the house.

His muscles tensed. Early had been able to leave them one clue, and the chances of another were slim to none. If Meyer moved Jenna again, the odds of losing her forever increased exponentially.

He rose slightly, itching to move in. He couldn't fail

this time. He couldn't let someone die while he was in saving distance. The stakes had been high enough and devastating enough the last time.

This time he might not survive because the victim was more than an acquaintance…it was the woman he loved.

"We can't let them leave." He spoke low into his radio, hoping to convey urgency, straining not to shout his insistence.

"Hold position." Nance's voice was firm, brooking no argument.

Wyatt glanced to his left and his right. Somewhere concealed in the trees at the front of the house were Chief Thompson and Officer Mike Owens. A couple of Mountain Springs officers and Agent Nance were all Jenna had. By the time the hostage rescue team arrived and got into place, she'd be gone.

The SUV pulled close to the door, blocking the view the agents had of the front of the house. From Wyatt's position, he had a clear view of both front and back doors.

Meyer appeared on the small front porch, dragging Jenna alongside him.

They were moving.

If Meyer wanted her dead, he wouldn't bother changing locations. Either he'd discovered she wasn't Amy and was planning to use her as bait to reel in her sister or…

Or he had much worse plans for her.

His grip on his pistol tightened. They had to move.

Now. If they lost Jenna, she could survive, but in a fate worse than death could ever be.

Nance had to see the consequences. Had to know them.

Wyatt clenched and unclenched his fists. *Come on...* He had no control. None. Jenna's life was in someone else's hands and all he could do was wait for an order that might never come.

Lord, if You can save her, please... Because Wyatt couldn't. He never could. Her life was in hands bigger than his.

Jenna was fighting with all she had, slowing Meyer as they crossed the small porch.

Two gunshots rang out in quick succession. Meyer dropped to the porch, dragging Jenna with him as the two tires closest to the porch rapidly deflated.

Someone in the house had fired on the SUV?

Early. He must still be inside.

The man in the driver's seat fired toward the house as a volley of shots came from the woods, placing Jenna in the cross fire.

Two more shots came from inside the house, then two men ran out the back, firing into the woods, shouting. Someone there had been spotted.

The driver of the SUV was firing volleys toward the woods in front of the house, preventing the chief and Owens from moving from their positions.

Meyer ran straight toward Wyatt, dragging Jenna with him.

This was it. His one chance to save her.

With one last quick prayer, Wyatt eased out of his secure position as Meyer dragged Jenna toward him.

The other man froze, planted his feet and pulled Jenna between himself and Wyatt.

Jenna's eyes widened. Fresh bruises marred her jaw and cheek, fueling Wyatt's anger. Relief mingled with the fear on her face. But when Meyer jabbed a pistol into her side, she froze.

Wyatt leveled his aim on Meyer's head, praying someone near the house would see what was going on and engage.

They likely wouldn't. It would be too easy to hit Jenna from such a distance. It was the same reason Wyatt couldn't risk a shot now. Jenna could not be this close to rescue only to end up becoming collateral damage.

Wyatt swallowed his fear for her and prayed his voice would be firm. "You won't get far dragging her through the woods with you. Let her go."

"And hand over my leverage?" Meyer was cocky, unwilling to admit he'd been bested already. His attitude made him twice as dangerous. "Forget it."

Wyatt held his gun level and tried another tactic. "You think you can survive in these woods? You grew up in the city. Lived in the city your whole life. You don't know these mountains. All sorts of creatures live out there. You have no food, no water... And you'll have me dogging your steps all the way. You won't last the night."

A shadow of doubt crossed Meyer's features, but he tightened his hold on Jenna, jabbing the pistol deeper into her rib cage until she gasped at the pain.

Wyatt had never wanted to beat a man so badly in his

life. If he could get one blow to that man's solar plexus, he could drop him like...

One blow. Hope surged through Wyatt. With gunshots still ringing from the house, help wasn't coming from anyone on the police force or the FBI.

But help might come from Jenna herself.

Jenna, who'd been taught to fight for herself by the one man who'd ever treated her like a daughter.

Wyatt made eye contact with her, forcing her to keep looking at him, praying silently she'd understand. "Meyer, you're a city boy. You probably *fight like a girl.*"

Meyer spoke but Wyatt didn't process the words, because Jenna's eyes suddenly cleared, smoothing from fear to gritty determination.

He'd gotten through. Jenna heard him loud and clear. She shifted her stance slightly, lifting her hands slowly as if surrendering. "I'll go with you. But please... Don't hurt anyone else. Please. And let Brian's sister go. He did what you asked."

Now he heard *her* loud and clear. *Don't shoot to kill if you want to find Brian's sister.* Nina Early was in danger. Her brother was being blackmailed to help Meyer and his crew.

Another gunshot cracked from the house.

Meyer's grip on Jenna slackened at the sound, the gun shifting.

Pivoting, Jenna drove her finger into Grant Meyer's eye, then dropped to the ground and rolled as he bellowed.

Wyatt fired.

Jenna screamed as Grant Meyer fell beside her, gun falling uselessly to the ground, blood seeping from his shoulder. She rushed to Wyatt, hands and knees crunching dead leaves as she scrambled to her feet.

He kicked the pistol out of reach, then reached for Jenna, keeping one eye and his pistol on Meyer as he drew her near.

"I'm on him." Brian Early's voice came from the direction of the house. He stepped forward deliberately, pistol trained on Meyer with one hand, while the other arm cradled against his stomach, blood seeping through his shirt from a wound on his shoulder. His face was drawn white with pain, but his expression was tight and determined. "You take care of Jenna."

"Your sister?" Jenna's voice shook, and she kept her head in Wyatt's shoulder.

"We'll find her next. And if he lied about where she is, we'll ask again. He'll tell us." Early toed Meyer's shoulder, eliciting a moan and a rough curse. "He's in no position not to."

Wyatt pulled Jenna closer, pressing his lips to her hair, keeping a wary eye on the two men before him. Just in case.

And then the clearing was flooded with vehicles, the silence shattered as the hostage rescue team spilled into the clearing, armed to the teeth and ready to put an end to the chaos.

Wyatt holstered his weapon, wrapped both arms around Jenna and held her close, her heart beating against his chest.

She was finally safe.

SEVENTEEN

Jenna stared at the fireplace in her apartment, a blanket wrapped around her shoulders, the silence deafening.

She was safe. There was no one else coming for her. It was over.

In spite of the truth, her brain wouldn't turn off the alarm bells or stop screaming the need for flight. Less than a week of fearing for her life and this sense of paranoid urgency had somehow become a new normal she hadn't expected to escape.

About fifteen minutes earlier, Jenna had convinced Erin, Jason and Shelley to leave her alone for a bit. She needed time to process.

They'd argued at first but eventually left the apartment, although Jenna was pretty certain they were either downstairs in the coffee shop or at the foot of the stairs standing unnecessary guard duty.

She'd needed the space, just for a minute. She'd spent the entire night in a whirlwind, first at the hospital, then in an interview with the FBI and Homeland Security, then with a crisis counselor. It had been days since she'd had time alone, and she craved it.

Except…she didn't.

Silence and solitude weren't what she needed. The only thing that was going to make her world right again was Wyatt.

Everything had happened so fast at Brian Early's cabin. They'd been separated almost as soon as the federal agents arrived, and she hadn't seen him since. Hours. All night. Every time someone new had entered the room, her heart had jumped, hoping it was him.

It never was.

There was no telling how long he'd be working with the aftermath of her kidnapping and the gun battle at Early's cabin. They'd asked her questions until her head spun, and she was a civilian. What would they ask of Wyatt?

She laid her head on the couch and stared at the ceiling, then closed her burning, sleep-starved eyes. He'd come. She had no doubt.

Maybe he'd even bring news about Amy.

With Meyer in custody and Logan dead, would her sister be free to come out of hiding? Would she even want to? Jenna had lived with terror for a few days. Amy had been running for three years. Detoxing from a life in hiding would take time.

Her sister deserved to be free. She was a hero. She'd put her life on the line to rescue the women Grant Meyer had traded like property, assigning them monetary value.

Value.

It was what Wyatt had been trying to tell her before, when they were hiding. She had value that exceeded this world. Sure, she'd accepted Christ, but she hadn't really let Him love her. She'd let men assign her value as easily as Grant Meyer had done, had measured herself next to others, had found herself wanting because of the way other people had behaved. The Matthew verse... God cared about the birds, and she was more valuable than them.

Because God loved her. God assigned her value, not a monster like Grant Meyer. Not her mother. Not even herself.

God.

The same God who spoke everything she saw and heard into being loved *her*. Even at her worst, when she'd tangled her life with Logan's, He'd loved her. He'd taken care of her.

Her eyes burned with unshed tears. He'd taken care of her using every means He had, even a known criminal like Anthony.

And a man like Wyatt.

Neither of them were perfect, but Christ had valued her enough to die for her.

And Wyatt had valued her enough to stare down death for her, too.

Jenna breathed in a peace, an assurance she'd never known before. Life wasn't perfect. Men weren't perfect. But her value didn't come from them.

It came from Christ.

And even though she wasn't perfect and Wyatt wasn't perfect...he cared about her. For the first time in her life she knew...she was worthy of being loved.

Two swift knocks at the door lifted her head. Her name came softly behind them.

Wyatt.

Jenna was at the door before she realized she'd moved, pulling it open without even asking for clarification.

And there he stood. Freshly showered. Blue jeans and a gray sweater doing everything to make him look perfect.

To make him look all Wyatt.

All hers?

He stood there, one hand behind his back, blue eyes locked on hers for a time that seemed to stretch into forever yet was not nearly long enough.

Jenna tilted her head, overcome by a shyness she couldn't explain. She stood in front of a man who had saved her life by risking his own and who now completely held her heart in his hands. His hands... "What are you hiding behind your back?"

A soft smile tipped his lips and he lifted his hand, extending a to-go cup from downstairs. "I wasn't sure if you'd made any or not."

Jenna's lower lip trembled as she accepted the gift. Tears pressed at her eyes as she looked at the cup. No, they hadn't talked about the stellar, toe-curling kiss. They hadn't talked about their pasts or their futures or anything. But she knew exactly what he was telling her. His feelings were on display in a large paper cup, the same as they had been while she sat in an apartment in Asheville, wondering where he was and what he was thinking.

He'd found a way to tell her.

She'd found a way to believe him.

She sniffed, then lifted her gaze to his, giving him a watery smile. "I love you, too."

Wyatt's cell buzzed. His gaze skipped to the side then returned to Jenna's. Without looking away, he pulled the phone from his pocket. "Ten six, Chief." The words tilted on a mischievous smile as he killed the call.

Like the first night he'd been in her home. *I'm in the middle of something and can't be interrupted unless the world's about to explode.* Jenna's stomach looped. Oh, please. No interruptions now, not with him looking at her like that.

He slipped the phone in his pocket and the coffee from her hand, set the cup on the table by the door and moved fully into the room, drawing her to him as he did. As he kicked the door closed behind him, he pulled her close, wrapping his arms around hers and finding her lips in a kiss she hoped would never end, one that said everything his gift to her had said and so much more.

She was breathless when he pulled away, then pressed his forehead to hers.

Seemed he was, too. "So…" He cleared his throat. "Looks like we have something to talk about."

"Like what?" If he kept looking at her this way, she'd talk to him about anything he wanted.

He inched back, searching for an answer. "Genevieve? Eve? Or Jenna?"

"Does it matter?" Her heart pounded.

"Definitely. Because one day, fairly soon, I think…" He swept the hair from her forehead, his eyes following his fingers as he tucked the lock behind her ear in a gesture of protection no man had ever lavished on her before. "I plan to ask one of those women to marry me. I'd love to know which one."

The thrill of him ran from the top of her head straight through to her toes, curling into the hardwood. Suddenly, it did matter. It mattered a lot. "Jenna."

His eyebrow arched in a question as his lips went to hers again, asking for permission.

"None of the others knew you," she whispered, meeting him halfway, sealing their future with the truth of exactly whom she was meant to be.

* * * * *

If you enjoyed Mistaken Twin,
look for these other stories by
Jodie Bailey: Dead Run, Calculated Vendetta
and Fatal Response.

Dear Reader,

Thank you so much for joining me for Wyatt and Jenna's story! It has been an interesting one to write. Jenna even kept a few secrets from me until she was ready to tell. So did her sister, Amy, whom you will get to meet in the next book!

Sadly, too many of us feel like Jenna—unwanted, unlovable, broken. That's one of the reasons I love Matthew 10:29-31, which was the driving verse for this book: "Are not two sparrows sold for a farthing? and one of them shall not fall on the ground without your Father. But the very hairs of your head are all numbered. Fear ye not therefore, ye are of more value than many sparrows." I also love Psalm 139, where it talks about God knowing all of the days of our lives before we were born, loving us so much that He *wrote them down.* I don't know about you, but that makes me feel safe, protected by the Father who created me. Trivia bit—if you read Erin and Jason's story in *Fatal Response*, you can see how Psalm 139 plays into that one, too.

This is what I want you to know, what I'm desperate for you to know if you don't already—God loves you. He loves you so big that He has even counted the number of hairs on your head—also Matthew 10. You might feel alone. You might feel like Jenna does—wholly unlovable. But that is never true. It has never been true. Whether you know Him or not, God loves you and He has already set up a way for you to know Him. I'd love it if you took a minute to ponder those verses in Matthew or if you went to Psalm 139 and saw His love for you firsthand.

Truly, my prayer is that this book and others like it will not only entertain you, but will also lead you to the truth of how fully you are loved.

Stop by and visit me at www.jodiebailey.com and let me know how you're doing. I'd love to hear your God story!

Jodie Bailey.

Get 4 FREE REWARDS!

We'll send you 2 FREE Books plus 2 FREE Mystery Gifts.

Love Inspired® Suspense books feature Christian characters facing challenges to their faith... and lives.

FREE Value Over $20

YES! Please send me 2 FREE Love Inspired® Suspense novels and my 2 FREE mystery gifts (gifts are worth about $10 retail). After receiving them, if I don't wish to receive any more books, I can return the shipping statement marked "cancel." If I don't cancel, I will receive 4 brand-new novels every month and be billed just $5.24 each for the regular-print edition or $5.74 each for the larger-print edition in the U.S., or $5.74 each for the regular-print edition or $6.24 each for the larger-print edition in Canada. That's a savings of at least 13% off the cover price. It's quite a bargain! Shipping and handling is just 50¢ per book in the U.S. and 75¢ per book in Canada.* I understand that accepting the 2 free books and gifts places me under no obligation to buy anything. I can always return a shipment and cancel at any time. The free books and gifts are mine to keep no matter what I decide.

Choose one: ☐ **Love Inspired® Suspense Regular-Print** (153/353 IDN GMY5)   ☐ **Love Inspired® Suspense Larger-Print** (107/307 IDN GMY5)

Name (please print)

Address   Apt. #

City   State/Province   Zip/Postal Code

Mail to the **Reader Service:**
IN U.S.A.: P.O. Box 1341, Buffalo, NY 14240-8531
IN CANADA: P.O. Box 603, Fort Erie, Ontario L2A 5X3

Want to try 2 free books from another series? Call 1-800-873-8635 or visit www.ReaderService.com.

*Terms and prices subject to change without notice. Prices do not include sales taxes, which will be charged (if applicable) based on your state or country of residence. Canadian residents will be charged applicable taxes. Offer not valid in Quebec. This offer is limited to one order per household. Books received may not be as shown. Not valid for current subscribers to Love Inspired Suspense books. All orders subject to approval. Credit or debit balances in a customer's account(s) may be offset by any other outstanding balance owed by or to the customer. Please allow 4 to 6 weeks for delivery. Offer available while quantities last.

Your Privacy—The Reader Service is committed to protecting your privacy. Our Privacy Policy is available online at www.ReaderService.com or upon request from the Reader Service. We make a portion of our mailing list available to reputable third parties that offer products we believe may interest you. If you prefer that we not exchange your name with third parties, or if you wish to clarify or modify your communication preferences, please visit us at www.ReaderService.com/consumerschoice or write to us at Reader Service Preference Service, P.O. Box 9062, Buffalo, NY 14240-9062. Include your complete name and address.

LIS19R

SPECIAL EXCERPT FROM

Love Inspired
SUSPENSE

When her son witnesses a murder, Julia Bradford and her children must go into witness protection with the Amish. Can former police officer Abraham King keep them safe at his Amish farm?

Read on for a sneak preview of
Amish Safe House *by Debby Giusti,*
the exciting continuation of the
Amish Witness Protection miniseries,
available February 2019 from Love Inspired Suspense!

"I have your new identities." US marshal Jonathan Mast sat across the table from Julia in the hotel where she and her children had been holed up for the last five days.

The Luchadors wanted to kill William so he wouldn't testify against their leader. As much as Julia didn't trust law enforcement, she had to rely on the US Marshals and their witness protection program to keep her family safe. No wonder her nerves were stretched thin.

"We're ready to transport you and the children," Jonathan Mast continued. "We'll fly into Kansas City tonight, then drive to Topeka and north to Yoder."

"What's in Kansas?"

Jonathan pulled out his phone and accessed a photograph. He handed the cell to Julia. "Abraham King will watch over you in Kansas."

Julia studied the picture. The man looked to be in his midthirties with a square face and deep-set eyes beneath dark brows. His nose appeared a bit off center, as if it had been broken. Lips pulled tight and no hint of a smile on his angular face.

"Mr. King doesn't look happy."

Jonathan shrugged. "Law enforcement photos are never flattering."

Her stomach tightened. "He's a cop?"

"Past tense. He left the force three years ago."

Once a cop, always a cop. Her ex had been a police officer. He'd protected others but failed to show that same sense of concern when it came to his own family. The marshal seemed oblivious to her unease.

"Abe is an old friend," Jonathan continued. "A widower from my police-force days who owns a farm and has a spare house on his property. He lives in a rural Amish community."

"Amish?"

"That's right."

"Bonnets and buggies?" she asked.

He smiled weakly. "You'll be off the grid, Mrs. Bradford. No one will look for you there."

Looking for inspiration in tales of hope, faith and heartfelt romance?

Check out **Love Inspired®** and **Love Inspired® Suspense** books!

New books available every month!

CONNECT WITH US AT:

Facebook.com/groups/HarlequinConnection

 Facebook.com/HarlequinBooks

Twitter.com/HarlequinBooks

Instagram.com/HarlequinBooks

Pinterest.com/HarlequinBooks

ReaderService.com

Love Inspired®

LIGENRE2018R2